To all the souls who suffered during the Salem Witch Trials and in the Old World.

Table of Contents

THE SALEM WITCH

HAYDEN BLACK
AND THE
SALEM WITCH TRIALS

PREQUEL NOVELLA

B.C. TAYLOR

NOSLRAC PUBLISHING, LLC

Copyright Page

The Salem Witch

Published by Noslrac Publishing, LLC

Copyright 2023 B. C. Taylor

Cover designed by B. C. Taylor using Canva A.I.

All rights reserved. No part of this publication may be reproduced in any form or by any means whatsoever without written permission from the author, except for brief quotations embodied in critical articles or book reviews.

This book is a work of fiction. Though some actual towns, cities, and locations may be mentioned, they are used in a fictitious manner and any names, characters, events and occurrences are a product of the imagination of the author. Any similarities of characters or names used within to any person, past, present, or future, are coincidental.

ISBN 978-1-959090-32-8

Library of Congress Control Number: 2024905929

First Edition paperback 2024

Noslrac Publishing

authorBCtaylor@gmail.com

brooklynctaylor.com

Reading Order

The Lost Witch

The Dark Mother

The Nephilim's Glory

The Earth's Curse

The Warrior Witch

The Salem Witch... Prequel Novella

CHAPTER ONE

FORBIDDEN MAGIC

Magic was forbidden.

1685 was not the time to be a witch. Especially not the Nephilim-witch daughter of Uriel, the Archangel of Earth.

But Alice Corey could not deny the identity of her mother any more than she could ignore the vast magical power that sang with life in her veins, aching to be released.

Seven years. Alice had held that magic in for seven years.

Or most of it, anyway.

The other villagers were not aware of her midnight magical activities, or the way she tilted her head from time to time to make a breeze blow through her waist-length, fiery red hair.

Alice glanced up from the snow-covered path she walked to see the backs of her mother's and father's heads. Her *adoptive* parents. She certainly had not inherited her hair from either of her parents, nor her dark hunter green eyes. Alice and her parents shared none of the same facial features, so she knew long before Martha told her last summer that she was adopted.

Little did they know, she remembered her mother. She remembered Uriel, in all her heavenly glory, who had descended to Earth, temporarily of course, to conceive, birth, and raise her one and only daughter.

Alice.

Celestials like Uriel could only have one mortal born child. But Heaven's rules could be cruel, because Alice was not allowed to live with her mother, who resided in the Heavens. Alice was ten years old now, and her mother left her with Martha when she was three.

Of course, she knew Giles was not her biological father, as Martha raised her alone for the better half of six years before marrying Giles. Giles and Martha married recently, but Alice grew up with Giles watching over her, as her parents were friends long before their romance began. But Giles's willingness to adopt Alice and give her his last name raised suspicion amongst the townspeople, who believed Alice to be Giles's illegitimate child, conceived out of wedlock. Not that it stopped them from gossiping about the possibility of her being the child of a different man.

Martha and Giles Corey were good but stern parents. Alice loved them, but sometimes she wondered why her mother, Uriel, entrusted Alice to them, in Salem of all places. Alice was *Nephilim*.

Nephilim were the half-mortal descendants of celestials like angels and gods and goddesses, who were manifestations of the magic of the one and only Creator. And the Creator was comprised of the Divine Masculine and the Divine Feminine—also known as God, who was worshipped by humans, and Goddess, who was worshipped by witches. As half-angel, Nephilim were part magic, and because of that, their magic was stronger than any other mortal's.

Magic was as natural as breathing to Alice, but Martha and Giles were adamant about one thing for their daughter—that she did *not* use magic. The very thing that made her unique, even from other witches.

Why would Uriel doom Alice to a magic-less life in Salem? Then again, Alice did not understand how she could be the daughter of the Archangel of Earth and an *air* witch.

Seven years. Only seven more years and Alice would be an adult witch, and she could leave Salem. She could travel the world and find somewhere safe for witches to freely practice their magic. Not

Europe. No, certainly not Europe. Men and women alike were dying by the thousands in the Old World, falling to the crazed men hunting for witches.

They were correct, of course, about the existence of witches, but their absurd manual for identifying a witch, *the Malleus Maleficarum*—the Hammer of Witches—could not be more inaccurate. Still, the horrors committed there... Alice shuddered. She prayed the Creator would end the torment. So many lives needlessly lost to men who feared what they did not understand. Those vile humans were the reason witches used magic to wipe the existence of witches from human memory all those centuries ago. Though the blanket spell cast over the world did not entirely erase all traces of magic, and some humans possessed minds of steel that were not easily changed.

But if Europe was not safe, and the New World was not safe, then where could Alice go?

Alice sighed, shaking her head so her red locks swung behind her as her parents led the way into town.

Colors of nature were dull and boring, depressing almost, as they painted the town. There was no greenery, no life in the midst of the cold winter day, and Alice missed the heat dreadfully.

The only exciting part of winter were the holidays, but with the Salem witches living in secret, they no longer celebrated Sabbats or Equinoxes. There was hardly any celebration, other than attending Mass on Christmas or perhaps honoring the Saints on All Saints' Day.

There was no Yule celebration for the Winter Solstice or festival for Samhain—the witch's new year when the veil between this world and the next dropped, allowing spirits to cross into the realm of mortals once more.

The trees were barren, the branches reaching into the overcast sky like fingers clawing for the sun, and Alice, too, yearned for those warm summer days. If she possessed the power, she would create a natural sanctuary for herself, an escape where it stayed summer year-round so she could enjoy all nature had to offer whenever she desired.

Salem was not an easy place to live, particularly during the cold months, but the villagers made do, even the ones without magic. Ramshackle houses, shoddily thrown together, dotted the horizon. Few were built with care, sturdy enough to endure the harsh winter to come.

Humans milled around the village, roaming from shop to shop, exchanging goods and money, bartering for deals, and engaging in lively conversation with one another, all the while ignorant of the witches in their midst.

Because Alice was not the only one forbidden from using magic. The Athenian Council—the governing body composed of seven witches elected to lead a magical community—outlawed magic for all witches in Salem. Every witching community had one, including Salem. It had been a decade since Salem's Council had formally assembled, when they banished a witch who actively used her magic. They allowed fear to dictate their lives, too afraid of discovery to accept their magic.

Even the Supreme Council, whom every Athenian Council in the world reported to, were hesitant to practice, instead urging witches to be cautious during these times and deny themselves and the magic born into them. And the Supreme Council resided in Jerusalem, which was not plagued by the fear of witch hunts like the Old and New Worlds.

As Alice followed her parents, winding through the crowded street toward the butcher shop, Alice knew the humans around her were oblivious to the magic running through her veins, through the veins of the witches they spoke to, the witches they attended church with. After all, humans and witches worshipped the same Creator, but while humans focused on the Divine Masculine, witches were created by the Divine Feminine, and thus worshipped the Goddess.

A breeze blew through the town, the wind stinging with cold November air. Alice repressed a shudder, drawing her wool coat tighter around her body. She fought the urge to use her magic, knowing if she did, that other, stronger witches may sense the flow of energy, and she would face the consequences doled out by the Athenian Council.

If she were allowed to, she could simply will the wind to divert its direction to either side of her. Unlike other witches, Alice required neither wand nor movement to channel her chi—energy or life force. She could direct the element with her thoughts alone.

She chalked up her ability to the blood of angels flowing through her veins, strengthening her magic beyond that of any other mortal. Except a Salem Witch, but it had been centuries since one had been born, and the likelihood of one appearing now... Alice wished the Creator would send one to save those people in Europe. To save the New World from devolving to such lows as to murder one another simply because they were *afraid*. Spineless cowards.

Alice detested the Athenian Council and their no magic rule. They reacted to their fear, giving the Devil what he wanted. And what he wanted was to use their fear against them such that mortals made decisions that benefitted him. And not using magic, magic gifted by the Creator, was like hiding one's face from the God and Goddess in shame.

It infuriated Alice to no end.

But her thoughts were left outside with the wind when she stepped across the threshold into the butcher's shop, staying close to her mother's skirts and diverting her eyes to the ground to avoid eye contact with the humans in the shop.

Alice often avoided eye contact with humans. Her fiery red hair stood out enough. She did not wish to draw more attention to herself with her unique hunter green eyes, dark as the forest. When she was younger, the townspeople pointed out the strangeness of her features, which she clearly had not inherited from Martha and Giles, as they both sported plain brown eyes. Martha's hair was the color of dirty straw while Giles's balding head sported straggly sandy brown strands, and Martha's previous husband had blond hair and brown eyes, features their daughter should have inherited, as they were dominant traits.

When Uriel entrusted Alice to Martha, the archangel cast a spell over the town, altering their memories, so all of Salem believed Alice to be Martha's biological child with her previous husband. However, it did not stop the humans from speculating an affair on Martha's behalf. Alice heard the whispers, the wind affectionately carrying their whispers to her. Her element often acted of its own accord, always loyal to her since the day she manifested powers on her third birthday. Both witches and humans suspected her to be a bastard. Many speculated Giles to be her actual father, despite his marriage to his second wife, Mary Blight, at the time Alice was conceived, which only made the rumor that much more scandalous. But others, especially those in the witching community, suspected she was born from a man who was neither Giles nor Martha's now deceased husband. Where else did her strange features come from?

"Serpents always lack a spine," the butcher growled. The butcher, a large human man with a barrel chest and bulging muscles under his blood-stained leather apron, stood behind the counter, his hands braced on top as he conversed with Martha and Giles. "That vile bastard is no better. Him and that weasel, Corwin. Mark my words, this election is only the beginning. If those two gain any more power, we shall suffer. I would sooner kill the serpents and take the hanging as punishment than bow to Hathorne and Corwin."

Alice raised her head at his clipped tone. The butcher was always kind to her family, so his harshness was startling.

The butcher scowled, but when his light blue eyes met Alice's hunter green ones, his expression softened.

"Best to discuss another time...." he muttered. "Politics are too dark to fall on the ears of a child."

Alice frowned, narrowing her eyes on the butcher, but he avoided her gaze, asking her parents what cut of meat they desired.

The wooden door behind Alice clattered open, the wind catching it and slamming the door against the wall. A biting current cut into the building, the stinging air sailing for Alice. The wind curled back on itself and shot out the door before it slammed into the Coreys.

Alice smiled a small smile. She did not ask her magic to redirect the wind. It simply acted in her best interest of its own accord.

What could she accomplish if she tried?

But Alice's mind did not linger on magic. Not when a young boy entered the shop behind his parents.

"Alice," John shouted her name in surprise, earning a "shh" from his mother, but he ignored her, hurrying to wrap Alice in a hug, pinning her arms to her side as he lifted her and spun her in a circle.

Laughter erupted from Alice's throat as he twirled her, despite him standing three inches shorter. As he embraced her, her magic rose to the surface of her skin, singing at the contact with John, a fellow witch.

While Alice was tall for a child of her age, taller than some of the older boys in the village, John never noticed how she towered over him. Perhaps it was because his magic seemed to spark to life within him at her presence, just as hers did in reaction to him. Alice's magic was never as alive around other witches as it was around John, and he said the same was true for him. Perhaps because there were not many witch children in the town, except Benjamin Nurse and his siblings. The Nurse family were agreeable people, and Alice liked Benjamin well enough, yet Alice would always choose John's company before theirs.

He set her on her feet, grinning at her with his twinkling hunter green eyes. Another thing Alice loved about John. His eyes were the same color as hers. While Alice inherited hers from her mother, the Archangel of Earth, John's were more of a mystery. Neither his mother nor father had green eyes, but with the way his magic reacted to hers, Alice wondered if John had the favor of her mother, Uriel.

"Do you want to skip rocks with me at the beach?" John asked, bouncing on the balls of his feet, his fingers crossed at his sides as though he worried Alice would deny him.

How silly of him to think such a thing. John was Alice's most treasured friend. She would never deny herself time with him.

"In this weather?" John's mother scoffed. "It is frigid out there, children, especially by the water."

Martha was engaged in conversation with the butcher as he wrapped the family's purchase in cloth, but Giles had been listening to the children, and with a warm smile, said, "They will be fine for a while. Children are too busy enjoying life to be bothered by the weather." With a wink at Alice, Giles said, "Go on. Your mother and I will be running errands for the rest of the day. Be home by supper."

Alice beamed with the light of the sun as she excitedly yelled, "Thank you, Giles."

Spinning on her heel, she grabbed John by the hand and pulled him outside into the bitter November air. Giles was right. The wind did not bother her so much as she ran through the streets with John nipping at her heels.

Salt stung Alice's nose before she broke through the tree line, and a certain peace settled over her. Massive waves swelled, then crashed on the shore, the sound soothing Alice's soul.

She paused, closing her eyes and inhaling a long, slow breath through her nose. Peace. The ocean soothed her soul in a way that air never did. Again, she wondered how, of all the elements, air was hers. Her personality was not like the other air witches at all—socially energetic, flighty, yet intellectual. Highly logical, they were the strictest about not risking magic use, while Alice was convinced she could practice magic secretly, without other witches noticing. Alice had a shrewd and cunning mind, but she did not consider herself a scholar like most air elementals.

Not that Alice was much of a fire witch, either. She liked to think she was fierce and courageous, but she was not a natural leader, nor was she impulsive. Although the Coreys likely disagreed with their daughter. Water elementals, like Martha, tended to be empathetic and intuitive, but could be easily traumatized because of their sensitive nature. Alice was not so easily rattled.

In all regards, Alice was an earth elemental—stubborn, sensible, steadfast, strong—except for the actual magic part.

Slowly releasing the breath she had been holding, Alice opened her eyes to find John browsing the shoreline, picking up stones that littered the sand, then tossing them aside if they did not meet his standards.

Alice lifted her skirts, exposing her bare legs to the cutting wind rolling off the ocean, and ran down the beach to search with John. The children roamed aimlessly, straying far and near one another in their search.

After accumulating a collection of stones in her apron, Alice returned to where John harbored his own small mound and dumped hers next to his.

John picked up the first rock, a flat white stone, and palming it, twisted his arm at an angle, then pulled it back before lashing it forward, releasing the stone. The stone skipped three times before it was swallowed by a wave.

"Ha," he shouted, a goofy grin splitting his face. "Beat that," he jeered triumphantly at Alice.

With a look of pure determination, Alice selected her rock, a solid sphere, the worst possible stone to skip. Alice rolled the rock between her pointer finger and thumb before suddenly twisting to sharply launch the rock through the air. The stone hit the water once, twice, thrice... four times before it, too, was swallowed by the ocean.

"Looks like this round goes to me," Alice taunted, but John beamed, his hunter green eyes swirling with an emotion Alice could not place but felt deep in her soul.

John bent to pluck another stone, then skipped it, this time only skipping the rock twice. Alice burst into laughter.

With a sigh, John shook his head, then swept his chestnut brown locks out of his eyes and gestured for Alice to throw. "Go on then, Alice. Let's see you best me again."

She grinned competitively at her friend. "Oh, I will."

Once more, Alice selected an odd stone from her pile, the rock fat and oddly shaped, completely different than the stones John strategically picked for their features that made them easily skip across the water. But Alice did not need to select a stone for its shape.

Why rely on skill when she could use *magic*?

Air swirled in her hand, nuzzling against her skin as she raised the rock to waist height. The stream of air wrapped around the misshapen rock, and as Alice pulled her arm back, then launched it forward, her magic shot forward with the rock, undetectable to the visible eye.

Her element soared, directing the stone according to her will as she focused her thoughts on the magic flowing from her palm. The stone hit the water once, then again and again, until it skipped five times, sinking into the ocean on the sixth.

John's mouth hung open, his hands splayed outward. "How?" he asked, his tone incredulous.

Alice merely chuckled at her friend's losing streak, her long red hair flying on the wind behind her as the air wrapped lovingly around her, like it enjoyed when she used her magic.

John was oblivious to her magic use. Magic was banished in Salem shortly before either of them were born, so he was not trained to sense energies like adult witches. He did not know how to manifest his own, only lock it away.

Alice's heart panged at the thought of John never letting his magic burrow through the earth or dance with the flames or blow with the wind or crash against the shore with the ocean waves. But Alice noticed the weeds under John's feet, struggling to grow through the rough sandy beach, seemed a little greener than the plants growing elsewhere. The flora reacted to him, feeding off the magic naturally wafting off his aura. It made her wonder... was John an earth elemental?

Unlike other witching communities where magic was not forcibly forbidden, Salem's Athenian Council supposedly destroyed the sorting crystal ball. An artifact used by witches for centuries for divination, yes, but also to sort witches into their elements—air, fire, water, or earth. Each witch could only possess the power of one element, except the Salem Witch, who could wield all four and the fifth element—Spirit.

John had never been sorted. And having never attempted magic, he did not know his element. But Alice knew hers. How could she deny the wind when it spoke so lovingly to her, when it answered her call from such loyalty? It protected her when she needed it.

Even as a ten-year-old child, Alice had a sharp mind, finding ways to invisibly integrate her magic into everyday life. Magic was, and always would be, part of who she was and who she was becoming. She could not change that aspect of herself any more than she could change her hunter green eyes.

She was torn between the girl she was and the woman she wanted to be. The *witch* she wanted to be.

"John." Alice watched as her last stone sank beneath the waves after skipping seven times. She turned to her friend, a serious expression claiming her features. "Have you ever thought what it would be like to practice—"

John leapt forward, covering her mouth with both of his hands. "Do not say it!"

Furrowing her brow, she swatted his hands away. "I was not going to say it," she retorted. "I was going to say I have been thinking about what it would be like if we did not have to *hide*." She emphasized the word with an exasperated sigh, something far too heavy to come from a ten-year-old child.

"We have to," John responded with a shrug. "It is how it has always been, and that is how it will always be."

"It was not," she argued. "We did not always hide our abilities. There was a time when we coexisted with humans. What if it could be that way again?" Light sparkled in her green irises.

John's expression was one of uncertainty. Hesitantly, he said, "I do not know, Alice…. I have heard my parents talk about the witch hunts in the Old World...." His whole body shivered. "It is scary what is happening there. If we have to hide to stay alive, then—"

"Is it really living if we are not being everything that we are?" Alice cut him off. She tugged at her vibrant red hair. "I mean, do you feel you are truly being yourself? I cannot help feeling like I am missing something, some big part of me."

John remained silent as Alice stared at the water, anguish written across her features. "Do you... do you think maybe you feel this way because your mother?"

A pained grunt came from the little girl as she hung her head. She lifted her eyes to meet John's matching green ones.

"Of course, John. My mother is supposedly the all-powerful Archangel of Earth, yet my element is air. How does that make any sense? I wish she would come explain it."

A deep chuckle came from behind the children, higher up the beach. John and Alice whirled around.

With fear and awe, the children stared at the seven-foot-tall angel as he strode forward, his white angel wings trailing behind him, cutting gouges into the sand. Stopping in front of Alice—her small, petrified body trembling in the angel's presence—he sat in the sand, as though he did not mind ruining his pristinely white clothes. Even sitting, he was as tall as Alice, his ocean blue eyes staring intently into hers.

Looking into those watery depths, Alice knew she had never truly seen ocean blue before. But his eyes were not like a normal human's or witch's. The pupils were entirely white, making his appearance all the more startling.

"Hello, Alice." He smiled warmly at her, but it did nothing to diminish his striking appearance, yet Alice could not help but like the angel despite her initial terror. "I am Gabriel, the Messenger Archangel, and a friend of your mother's."

John and Alice gawked at him, their jaws dropping open.

"Do you know why I am here?"

She snapped her jaw shut, then said, "Um, to deliver a message?"

Gabriel chuckled merrily. "Yes, Little Bull." The bull was Uriel's sacred animal, which made it Alice's sacred animal. It was the nickname her mother used to call her. One of the few memories Alice retained of her mother. "But today, I have a special message for you."

Alice's hunter green eyes lit up. "Is it from my mother?" she asked excitedly, bouncing on the balls of her feet.

"My purpose for appearing before you now is to deliver a message from the Goddess." Alice's face fell, her chin dipping low, but Gabriel continued talking. "But I do have a message from Uriel as well."

Alice's head snapped up, light shining from her face. At ten years old, all Alice wanted was to know her mother cared about her. That her mother did not discard her on Earth because the celestial could not be bothered to raise her mortal descendant.

"Okay, what is the message?" she demanded of the archangel.

With a chuckle, he patted her on the head. "First, I have come to tell you that you are a special witch, Alice Urielson Corey. Do you know of the Salem Witch?"

Alice nodded vigorously. "Yes, the Salem Witch is chosen by Heaven upon his or her birth to master all four elements, plus the fifth element, Spirit, which cannot be wielded by anyone other than the Salem Witch."

"Good." He nodded his approval. "And do you know why the Salem Witch must master the elements?"

"Because Salem Witches are only chosen when the world is on the brink of a war that cannot be won without a champion of Heaven fighting for peace."

"You are a smart witch, Alice. Uriel must be proud."

Alice beamed at his praise, bouncing on her toes with barely contained enthusiasm.

"Alice, I, the Archangel of Prophecies and the Messenger of the Heavens, have come to Earth to deliver a message from Heaven to witchkind." Gabriel placed one massive hand on the crown of Alice's head and the other gently wrapped around her tiny shoulder as he placed his palm over her heart. Power zapped over Alice's skin, tingling with the untold magic possessed by the angel. Her magic swelled inside her, swirling fast in her core, as though it wanted to reach out and touch Gabriel's magic.

"Upon your birth ten years ago, you were chosen by Heaven. A war is coming, one that Earth cannot possibly hope to win without you. This moment serves as the beginning of your journey. You have until the dawn of your seventeenth year to master all five elements and conquer the Salem Witch Trials. Should you fail, this realm will fall forever to Darkness. Only your soul can fulfill this task. You have the blessing of Heaven. Do not fail us."

Alice's eyes grew to the size of saucers, then snapped shut as blinding white light erupted where Gabriel's hands touched her forehead and heart.

A wall inside her shattered. Gabriel's light obliterated the shards, and power surged through Alice's veins, filling every fiber of her being—both her mortal body and her immortal soul. Power unlike anything she felt before tingled over her skin, begging her to unleash it.

John shielded his eyes from the blinding heavenly light, but when he lowered his arm, blinking, his eyes widened at Alice.

If this was the power of the Salem Witch, then her magic before—magic significantly stronger than any other witch's—was the power of a Nephilim. But combined... she raised a hand to stare at her palm, her eyes tracing the invisible magic dancing over her skin.

Gabriel gazed at Alice with a kind, fatherly smile. "I cannot stay in this realm for much longer, but before I go, I promised to deliver a message from your mother. Are you ready?"

Alice focused intently on Gabriel, her magic momentarily forgotten, and nodded, fierce determination instilling her soul as she acknowledged the truth of who she was—both Nephilim and Salem Witch, a rare combination.

"Uriel wants you to know her love for you is infinite as she could never love another more than she does you."

Tears welled in Alice's eyes before pouring down her cheeks. Her bottom lip quivered, and she pressed her lips together to swallow her silent sobs.

"Second," Gabriel continued. "Uriel wishes with all her heart that she could be the one to raise you here on Earth. It is unbearably painful for her to be separated from you." Alice nodded stiffly, the rivers running down her cheeks rushing faster. "Uriel is the Archangel of Earth, and you are the Nephilim of Earth, therefore, it will always protect you. Whenever you are in need, touch the Earth, and She will protect you. Even when you cannot feel her, your mother is watching over you. We all are." Gabriel used his thumbs to wipe away the tears staining Alice's cheeks. "Good luck, Alice, Daughter of Earth."

In another flash of brilliant white light, the archangel disappeared. Alice and John stared at the sand where Gabriel had been, both of them frozen in place.

John snapped his jaw closed and rushed over the few feet separating them to wrap Alice in the tightest embrace he could muster.

Shocked by the contact, Alice pulled away from him, her eyes wide and fearful as she searched his gaze. Her voice was frantic as she croaked, "Do not tell anyone."

Solemnly, he agreed, "You have my word, I will not utter a word of this."

With a sigh of relief, Alice sank into his embrace, squeezing him as tightly as he held her in the innocent way only a child could.

Alice held her hand out in awe.

She was the Salem Witch, the only witch who could wield all four elements. No. Five elements, if one included Spirit. But since Gabriel touched her... touched by an angel... Alice was literally touched by an angel... her powers magnified to far greater than they had been.

It was as though she could see the air slipping between her fingers rather than just feel it. The wind was not a normal breeze.... Alice could feel more than that.... She could sense the essence of the air.

Curling her hand into a fist, she grabbed hold of the air like it was a real, tangible object. She released a light gasp, unfurling her hand and releasing the wind.

Magic.

Alice laughed to herself.

By choosing her as the Salem Witch and granting her all the power that came with the title, the Creator gave Alice Its blessing to practice her magic. And no witch could argue with the word of the Creator.

"Watching you do that makes me nervous," John said from where he perched on a boulder.

They had rowed to the Misery Islands for privacy. The townsfolk of Salem would not go out of their way to explore the island, not without reason, and that made it the safest place for Alice to practice.

"You are only as touched by the magic of this world as you wish to be. You forget, John, air is invisible. No human can detect my magic. I do not need to move to command the air. Only a witch could sense the prana"—her life force or energy—"flowing through me to direct the winds. I assure you, we are perfectly safe here as I practice with this element."

"And the other elements?" John pressed.

With a sigh, Alice ceased the flow of her magic and turned to John. "I admit, fire will present a challenge, but water is subtle, for the ocean is a force of its own, and earth... nature forges its own course. Who is to say there is another force at work?"

John scoffed. "As if they need a reason to persecute witches in the Old World? If any human so much as gets a whiff of your magic, they will target you. I do not want to see you burn, Alice."

"And how will a human sense that I am the force blowing the breeze, John? I am as likely to be accused of witchcraft if I do not practice as I am if I practice with an invisible element in the privacy afforded by these islands. But if I do not practice, then it is certain that I will not master the element, and you know the rules as well as I. If I do not master the five elements before my seventeenth birthday, I will forfeit my life. Perhaps it will not be a hanging or a burning, but I will die nonetheless."

John stared at Alice, his hunter green eyes wide, as her words sank in, as though he was so blinded by his fear of detection that it did not occur to him that Alice was a slave to these Trials, like every Salem Witch before her. The angels dictated it so. By tying the Salem Witch's life to the Trials, Heaven ensured the witch's dedication to waging the war against evil. Whatever that evil may be.

It was a mystery to Alice, and while she did not know what evil entity she would face in her Salem War, she had the unsettling feeling in her gut that it had something to do with the witch hunts.

Gazing across the narrow stretch of ocean separating her from the mainland, Alice wondered how much worse the witch hysteria and fear would escalate in the next seven years.

Salem was untouched for now. But like a punch to her abdomen, intuition slammed into Alice, and she knew her people would not be safe for long. But her people were no longer just the witches of Salem, but the humans and witches of the world.

Seven years was all the time she had. No other Salem Witch in recorded history had mastered the elements so quickly. But Alice was no ordinary Salem Witch. She was the daughter of Uriel, the Archangel of Earth, and this was her domain. The creatures of earth had always belonged to her, but now... now she realized it was her responsibility to protect them from the impending darkness.

With unyielding determination, Alice summoned magic to her palm, commanding it to wrap around the air. Whipping her hand, she sent a slash of air sailing across the beach to plow against a boulder, the force of her magic throwing it into the ocean.

With a smug grin, Alice summoned her magic again.

CHAPTER TWO

A Breath of Fresh Air

A gust of wind blew around the island, circling faster and faster until a cyclone touched down, spewing sand. With a snap of her fingers, the whirlwind simply disappeared. Yet Alice had not yet triggered her Air Trial.

Two and a half years had passed since Gabriel declared Alice the Salem Witch. It was March of 1688, and Alice was nearly a master of air.

In her mind, there was nothing more to the element to master. Alice excelled with her magic, but apparently, the angels did not agree. It was beyond infuriating. How was she supposed to master the five elements and conquer her Trials before her seventeenth birthday? She did not have a teacher for air, nor would she have a guide for any of the elements, unlike Salem Witches in history's past. Yet none of those witches were tasked to complete their Trials in seven years. They had the luxury of being announced as the Salem Witch when they were born or as mere children.

Alice was only twelve, but she did not consider herself a child anymore. Not after Gabriel proclaimed her momentous destiny.

With a sigh, Alice silently motioned to John. Abandoning his subtle, almost fearful attempt to grow the plants edging the beach with his earth magic—for they had long since discovered he was an earth elemental when Alice's cyclone raged out of control and his magic surged to protect him by raising a wall of stone—John followed her to the dingy they used to row from the mainland to the Misery Islands.

Climbing in, Alice summoned a gentle breeze to push them as they rowed. The rowing was more for show than anything. If someone spotted the two adolescents, she did not wish to explain how the air miraculously blew them in the right direction.

After reaching the shore, Alice and John stashed their boat in an alcove hidden by jagged rocks and covered it with a blanket of moss and plants woven together, then made their way into town, as they always did after a session of magic practice during the day. If people saw them in town, none would suspect they were off performing magic. With the hysteria in Europe and growing mutterings around town, John was paranoid and Alice was cautious.

She could not shake the feeling that someone—or something—was watching her and that person had something to do with the increasing fear of witches and magic.

Ignoring John's rambling chatter, Alice spun in a circle, sweeping the area with her eyes and her magic. But she neither saw nor sensed any being other than herself and John.

With sharp and suspicious eyes, she lengthened her stride to keep up with John, who was oblivious to her paranoia. But something was out there. She could feel it.

John froze mid-step, his mouth agape with whatever he was saying. But Alice froze against her will. The breeze did not blow, nor did the plants rustle. As if time itself stopped.

"Hello, Alice," Gabriel's masculine voice rumbled as he appeared in a flash of white light. Uncanny blue eyes with a white pupil seemed to see straight to Alice's soul as the archangel read her mind.

Alice had grown since she last saw the archangel, but he still towered above her at seven feet tall, and his pristinely white wings seemed larger than life as they shielded his back.

"Your people are in grave danger. You must save the humans and witches alike if you are to pass your Air Trial, but today will not compare to the dangers to come. Good luck, daughter of Uriel."

Touching his hands to her heart and forehead, Gabriel pulsed white light into Alice's petite body, and a tingling sensation assaulted her scalp and eyes as she watched her fiery red locks turn to a metallic silver that glimmered as bright as the moon.

Gasping, Alice fell into motion beside John, stumbling to catch herself as he continued unfazed. The Messenger Archangel had disappeared with the light as time began again, as though it never stopped.

"What—Alice, are you—" John fell speechless as his eyes landed upon her new appearance.

Staring at him with wide, silver eyes, Alice whispered. "My Trial has begun."

Her words spurred him into action. "You cannot be seen. We must go home and hide."

"No, John. Gabriel said the town is in danger, and I am to protect it."

"Gabriel?" John's face twisted in confusion. "When did you talk to him?"

"Just now." Alice motioned to the spot Gabriel disappeared from. "It was as if the entire world stopped. You were paralyzed, as was I, but Gabriel moved freely. He initiated my Trial."

"But what are you to do? The humans cannot see you like this, or they will accuse you of sorcery."

Alice chewed her bottom lip. "I have heard of a type of spell. It is not elemental magic, but practical. The enchantment must be cast with a wand to rearrange one's appearance, so others see a mirage. It is called a Glamour Charm."

"But you do not have a wand. Only the witches who possessed them before magic was outlawed have a wand."

Alice looked to the woods lining the path they walked. Perhaps she did not own a wand, but she was the Nephilim of Earth, and that must count for something.

Confidently, she strode to a large white oak tree and placed a flat palm against the trunk. Closing her eyes, she spoke to the tree, knowing its spirit heard her.

"Ancient One, I am in need of your assistance," Alice beseeched. "As the Salem Witch and Nephilim of Earth, I call upon your spirit to aid me in my time of duress. I desire a wand, one strong enough to channel the power of my magic. Please, if you are willing, grant me a branch from your tree, so I may perform the magic to hide my identity from those who seek to harm me."

Something within the child witch stirred, awakening as she connected with the spirit of the tree. Although Alice could not wield earth magic yet, her soul knew the earth, and it knew her. It was a connection that could never be hidden, and she knew the old oak sensed it as well. The bark of the tree shifted under Alice's hand as the branches shook.

"Uh, Alice..."

She did not open her eyes to see what made John so uncertain, for she knew the branches of the tree were shifting, twisting, and rearranging themselves.

Alice held her empty hand in the air, and a smooth branch fell into her open palm. Power rang through her at the connection, and Alice knew in her soul that this wand would serve her for the rest of her life, for it was granted by Mother Nature herself.

"Thank you," she said, removing her hand from the trunk, then bowed to the tree. "I honor you and your ways."

Straightening, Alice raised the wand in her hand. It was magnificent. She could not have designed a more perfect wand herself. Swirling vines and leaves and flowers engraved the smooth wooden surface from the tip of the wand to the hilt, where the vines wrapped around a glowing emerald embedded in the base of the handle.

Grinning, Alice tapped the tip of the wand against the top of her head, willing her magic to take root. Imagining her normal appearance, she let her magic flow, picturing her long red hair and dark green eyes that would be seen by the rest of the world while she saw the silver pigment of her hair.

"Whoa," John breathed out the word. "That was incredible, Alice. You are a natural witch when it comes to performing new magic."

Blushing at the compliment, Alice tucked a lock of silver hair behind her ear and smiled at her feet. John had a knack of making her feel special, in a way that differed from others who made her feel like an outcast. But to John, she was a priceless gemstone where they saw an uncut slab of stone.

Taking him by the hand, she pulled him down the path, running into the town together. Laughing and giggling, Alice and John looked like two normal human children as they raced through the streets of Salem, no different from Benjamin Nurse and the young boys accompanying him when John and Alice came across them. Although the Nurses were witches in hiding, too.

Benjamin held a slingshot in one hand as he waved at John and Alice with the other.

"Hello, Benjamin," Alice greeted him, then nodded to the other boys as John spoke to them. "What are you doing?" She motioned to the slingshot in his hand.

Benjamin grinned playfully. "We are having a competition to see who can knock the tin off the log." He pointed down the alleyway to a can sitting atop a piece of rotted wood.

"May I have a go?" Alice asked, earning a snort from several of the other boys. Casting them a dark look, she expectantly held her hand out to Benjamin for the slingshot.

Glancing at the other boys, Benjamin handed the slingshot to Alice somewhat reluctantly.

A boy snorted again, crossing his arms over his chest. "As if a girl could beat us. Can you even pull the strap?"

The other boys snickered at this comment, adding insults to the conversation, but Alice ignored them as she stepped to the line drawn in the dirt. While these boys had been playing with slingshots, Alice had been practicing with air, and air was a far more versatile weapon than a simple, roughly hewn tool.

Squeezing one eye shut, she pulled the strap and aimed. With a sharp exhale, she released the strap, launching the pebble forward. Magic surrounded the projectile as it shot into the tin can, knocking it from the log with a clatter.

Silence fell upon the alley as the boys stared at her with astonishment. Benjamin regarded her with an impressed grin, oblivious to her magic use as he had never practiced his own.

Guffawing, the boy who insulted her earlier, said, "Lucky shot. Doubtful you could hit the can again."

John scurried down the alley to return the can to the tree stump. Accepting another stone from Benjamin, Alice aimed once more, then shot the rock through the air to knock the tin off the stump again, much to the astonishment and rage of the mean boys. Then she did it again and again, until no one could question her skill.

Wordlessly, Alice handed the slingshot to Benjamin with a wink, then took John by the hand and skipped down the alley, leaving those silly boys to their toys.

John cackled madly. "Brilliant, Alice! You showed them."

She smiled to herself. Yes, she certainly had. But her pride soon faded as she caught another glimpse of her silver hair.

Pausing in the middle of the street, Alice lifted a lock of silver hair and twisted it between her fingers... her Trial... she should not have been wasting time showing off to human boys. She should have been seeking her Trial—

Glass-shattering shrieks pierced the air as an animal roared from a block away. Alice and John spun toward the sound, holding one another tightly. Another animalistic growl reverberated through the air as the noises of chaos carried through the air to Alice's ears.

"Bobcat!" a man's voice rang out, cutting through the shrieks of the townspeople.

Alice shared an alarmed look with John, who grabbed her by the wrist and pulled her in the opposite direction of the shouts. Hiking up her skirts with one hand, Alice sprinted toward the edge of town and the road that led to her parents' estate.

"Gerald!" a woman screeched.

Grinding her heels into the dirt, Alice slid to a halt, yanking her hand from John's grasp as she spun to face the village.

"Alice, what are you doing?" John seized her hand again. "We have to run."

"No, John," she said savagely. She faced him, her silver eyes boring into him, though he could not see through her glamour. "The butcher is in trouble."

He had always been kind to Alice. Kinder than any of the other humans or witches in town. She would not see him harmed when she could save him.

"You cannot help him now."

"Yes, I can." She charged forward with John trotting at her heels. "This is my Trial. It is my duty to save him. Him and the others."

Breaking into a sprint, Alice practically flew to the center of town, the wind at her back urging her faster. Forgetting John, she surged ahead until she reached the town common in record time, but the townsfolk clogged the streets as they clawed at one another, stampeding in their desperate attempt to escape the wild beast.

How was Alice supposed to get to the town square?

"Alice," John called. "Over here." He raced into a side alley, beckoning her to follow.

Sprinting after him, Alice found John stacking rubbish from the alleyway—an empty crate placed atop an abandoned barrel.

"John, that will not hold," Alice reprimanded him for wasting her time.

"It does not need to," he shot back quietly. "It only has to look like we are using the items in case someone spots us. Use your air magic to lift us to the roof, and we can drop to the other side."

Alice grinned at her friend. "John, you are a genius." She grabbed him by the shoulder and planted a kiss on his cheek, then grabbed hold of the barrel, lifting herself with the help of her air magic, but moving as though she were actually climbing the unstable structure.

"John, are you coming?" she asked from the rooftop, startling him from his paralysis.

Why was he just standing there?

"What? Oh yes." He grabbed hold of the barrel as she had, and Alice silently summoned the wind to assist him.

Once they both stood on the roof, they raced to the other side of the building and dropped into the square below as the bobcat's razor-sharp claws shredded through the thatch roof of the butcher's shop on the opposite side of the square.

The town common was in chaos as witches and humans screamed in hysteria, the crowd pushing and shoving as the mortals scrambled to escape the attacking bobcat. Not that it cared when it could smell the raw meat inside the butcher's shop.

But it was a wild animal, and there was no telling what it would do.

The butcher laid face-down in the street, blood splattered on the gravel around his fallen body.

Alice's heart stopped in her chest. Reaching out with her magic, she prodded the man's vitals until she confirmed he was alive. Her breath left her in a rush as she sighed in relief. Alive, but abandoned by the townsfolk fleeing for their lives. But Alice would not abandon him.

In public, Alice could not use her magic openly, therefore, she must command her element telepathically. Without moving her body, she sent a squall smashing into the bobcat, throwing it against the brick chimney with a yelp before it could dive through the hole into the butcher's shop.

Oh Goddess. What did she do?

The bobcat rose to all fours, its golden eyes narrowing on her. It knew. Alice knew better—all animals possessed a sixth sense to detect the supernatural, including magic.

With its acute feline reflexes, the bobcat leapt from the roof of the shop, landing gracefully on the gravel street below.

"John, go!"

"But—"

"Get the people out of here while I fight. Now," she screamed as the bobcat rushed toward them. Shoving him out of the way, Alice squared off with the wildcat.

Air slammed into it from above, smashing it face-first into the ground.

John rushed to the edges of the square, shouting at the people as they bottlenecked around the mouth where the road met the square. It would do no good. Nobody listened while hysterical, but Alice wanted John out of harm's way.

The bobcat was on its feet.

Untying her apron from around her waist, Alice raised the soiled white cloth in front of her.

The cat charged her, swiping with its vicious claws. Alice dove out of the way, releasing the apron and summoning a gust of air to wrap the cloth around the bobcat's face as it ran into the garment.

Swatting at its face, the bobcat struggled to free itself from the cloth, but Alice had bought herself a few moments. But a shredded apron would not save her again, and there were too many people trapped in the town common. Frantically, she scanned the square. She needed a weapon... she needed a...

There!

Benjamin Nurse's slingshot lay abandoned in the dirt.

The bobcat lunged for her, its talons slashing. Throwing herself out of the way, Alice lurched for the slingshot while simultaneously pushing it toward her with a gust of air.

Hitting the ground, her hand wrapped around the handle.

The bobcat hissed, baring its fangs at her, and pounced. Rolling out of the way, Alice summoned a gust of wind to kick the bobcat into the side of a brick building. Its spine smacked against the corner, eliciting a cry of pain from the beast.

On her knees, Alice scrambled in the dirt, searching for a stone. She needed one sharp enough to hurt the bobcat.

But the bobcat had recovered and was prowling toward her, a threatening growl reverberating deep in its chest.

Alice scooped up a handful of pebbles at her feet, loaded them into the slingshot, and fired. The pebbles sprayed at the bobcat in a barrage, but it only enraged the wild cat.

It lunged for Alice, but she was not fast enough to dodge. A blast of air smashed into its side, throwing it off course for Alice to scurry to the side.

Tripping on a basket discarded in the street, Alice fell to her hands and knees, scraping the skin off her palms. The coppery scent of blood stung her nose as the rocks and dirt dug into her open flesh.

An enraged roar sounded behind her as the bobcat gnashed its canines.

"Alice, look out!" John shouted.

Alice dropped to the ground, pressing her body flat against the earth as she formed a wall of hard air with her magic and summoned another blast of air to throw the bobcat over her as it tried to jump onto her, its claws poised to shred her into pieces.

John's warning saved her life.

Still pressed into the ground, Alice's silver eyes landed on exactly what she sought. Inches from Alice's nose sat a hefty stone, big enough and sharp enough to inflict damage, but small enough to fit into the pouch of the slingshot.

Scrambling to her feet, Alice grabbed the stone.

The bobcat's golden eyes sliced into her as it snapped its jaws, hunting her as its prey. The bobcat charged.

Alice shoved the stone into the slingshot, positioning it so the sharp point faced outward. Raising the feeble weapon, she pulled the strap and aimed.

The bobcat moved in a blur, but with a calm inhale, Alice used her air magic to press against the deadly beast, slowing its attack.

The world seemed to slow around her as she exhaled, releasing the strap. Air swirled around the stone, increasing its velocity to an impossible speed for a girl without magic as the air directed the stone's trajectory.

Holding her breath, Alice watched in fear and hope as her stone rocketed toward the wild cat.

The sharp, jagged tip sank into the bobcat's eye, piercing the soft flesh and sinking into its brain from the force of Alice's magic.

With a wild shriek, the bobcat crumpled, its body still moving forward as it hit the ground and slid to a stop mere inches from Alice's toes.

The wild beast lay motionless at her feet.

Alice waited with bated breath, not daring to move as her magic stretched out from her, confirming the bobcat was dead.

A hushed silence blanketed the town square as the unlucky souls, who were stuck behind the throng of frantic people trying to escape, ceased their screaming to stare at her with wide eyes.

Appearing at her side, John threw his arms around Alice. "Thank God, you are alright."

Staring at the dead bobcat with wide eyes, Alice let the slingshot slip from her grasp to clattered against the gravel.

Mutterings erupted among the townsfolk. "She saved us..."

"That was a cunning way to fell the beast..."

"... how smart of her..."

"... alive because of the Corey girl."

Sighing in relief, Alice sank into John's embrace, letting him pull her into his chest. Her heart hammered in her chest as he took her by the hand and guided her out of the town, leaving the awe-struck townspeople behind. But Alice's mind was still spinning.

Was that her Air Trial? If it was, did she pass? Or was there more to come? Her hair was still silver—would Gabriel appear to change it back? All these thoughts and more swirled through her mind as they trudged down the abandoned path through the woods toward home.

Brilliant white light blinded Alice, and she threw up an arm to shield her eyes until the light faded. Blinking, Alice lowered her arm to reveal the Archangel Gabriel.

John's mouth hung open as he gawked at the seven-foot-tall angel, but Alice smiled at Gabriel, thrilled to see him again so soon.

"How did I do?" she asked.

"Congratulations, Little Bull," Gabriel said with a smug smile, those uncanny blue eyes cutting through Alice to her soul. "In showing fearlessness, intelligence, and sacrifice, you have passed your Trial of Air."

Pressing his right hand over her heart and his left to the crown of her head, white light beamed from Gabriel's hands, sinking into Alice's body so the magic of Heaven could unleash the fire burning in her belly.

Warmth spread through her rapidly as Gabriel's touch swept away the barrier obstructing her from accessing her next element. Green flames sprang to life in her hair as the locks changed from silver to fiery red, and her eyes returned to their normal hunter green.

Grinning, Alice summoned green flames to her curled fist, lifting it to stare into the flames.

At last, she was a master of air and a witch of fire.

"I am not so sure practicing with fire magic at night is wise," John said with a frown. "It would be less visible during the day."

"Perhaps," Alice semi-agreed. "But there are too many wandering eyes during the day, and we could be followed. But at night, few are out at this hour."

Two in the morning was a time for dark deeds. Only the craftiest and sneakiest of people were awake and moving. And that included John and Alice.

Misery Islands had long since been their midnight rendezvous spot for magic practice, but Alice unlocked her fire magic months ago when she passed her Air Trial, so she was a novice with fire, though progressing quickly despite training without a teacher to guide her.

"Still," John pressed, "green flames are a bit alarming, do you not think?"

Green was the color of Alice's magic, inherited from her mother, Uriel. Every time Alice saw her magic, even if it was in the form of flames, she felt more connected to the mother she did not know and barely remembered.

But she wanted more. She wanted to see her mother, not just hear her voice from time to time.

Alice held her palms flat up, summoning dark green flames to burn in her hands.

"I can summon the flame easily, like I could control the air without effort, but I do not know how to become a master," Alice said to John, ignoring his earlier question. "I am uncertain what triggered my first Trial, so I do not know what I am to learn with this element."

John shrugged. "Perhaps the Trial has less to do with you and more about the people."

Alice paused, cocking her head at him. "Whatever do you mean?"

"You said Gabriel said the town was in danger right before your Trial began. What does that have to do with you? It seems like it has more to do with the external circumstances of the people you are meant to protect."

Alice frowned, her mind whirling. "But I am supposed to master the element? If I do not, then I cannot start the Trial."

"Or maybe the Trial will happen either way, but if you do not train with the elements, you will not have the skill to pass."

"But while I await my Trial, how do I master the element of fire? I have no teacher, no guide, nor a fellow witch to learn alongside. It is as though the angels wish for me to fail."

John placed a hand on both of her shoulders and waited until she met his hunter green gaze. "The angels would not have set you up for failure, Alice. It is in the best interest of Heaven for you to succeed. You are more than capable of mastering the element on your own. In fact, I think another witch would hinder your natural ability. Trust your intuition, and it will not lead you astray." He pressed a kiss to her forehead, then released her and retreated several paces, gesturing for her to practice with her flames.

Letting her eyelids flutter closed, Alice tunneled into her gut where her magic swirled.

Trust her intuition?

Her intuition said fire was destructive and dangerous. It burned and consumed and devoured without end. Demons burned with perpetual hellfire and brimstone. It could rage out of control if unchecked, but it was *more*. It was life-giving. In the midst of the frigid winters, it drove the cold away. It cooked raw meat into food and was used in agriculture to slash and burn the fields to renew the soil.

There was so much more to fire.

It was the passion of the heart and the fierceness of a rage. And like a phoenix, it could burn one to the ground, cleansing one of their burdens so they may be reborn from the ashes.

After all, was Alice not reborn the day Gabriel claimed her as the Salem Witch on behalf of Heaven? Was she not transformed in the fires of baptism when her powers awakened? When they truly awakened with the might of Heaven?

White flames sparked to life, lovingly licking the skin of her palms. As her eyes snapped open, a light gasp escaped Alice's parted lips.

"White flames?" John asked, drawing nearer to inspect her hands. "I thought your magic was green?"

"It is," Alice confirmed, marveling at the fire she now held. "My magic does not color these flames because they are holy flames, John. I can summon the fire of the Heavens."

CHAPTER THREE

FIRESTORM

"Any idea what this is about?" John whispered to Alice as he slid into the seat next to her, his earthy musk overwhelming Alice's sense of smell.

Alice and John sat in the front pew of the church, their parents talking in hushed, somber tones only feet away.

Pews stretched across the church in rows, filling the hall, but at the back of the church, a sliver of space was dedicated to a simple altar, several ornate wooden crosses, and a pedestal with the Holy Grimoire—the witches' holy scripture.

Witches milled about the sanctuary and conglomerated in the pews, whispering conspiratorially, while more witches filtered into the church.

Alice's eyes flicked to Martha and Giles to make sure they were preoccupied talking with John's parents. The adults did not spare the nearly fifteen-year-old Alice and sixteen-year-old John a second glance. It had been years since Alice mastered her air magic, but the Coreys were none the wiser to Alice's progression to fire magic. In fact, Alice declined to ever inform them of her status as the Reigning Salem Witch. It would only place their lives in danger.

Reigning because she was the Salem Witch in the midst of her Trials. She only hoped she lived to become the Resigned Salem

Witch—when the Salem Witch had mastered the elements and ended her Salem War.

Somewhat bitterly, Alice admitted, "I have a few theories." She grimaced. "None of them are good. Especially not for *me*." She widened her hunter green eyes at him, emphasizing her meaning.

To this day, John was the only witch who knew her secret. He was probably the only other witch in Salem who used his magic, practicing alongside Alice, who learned through trial and error, having no experienced witch to guide her magic lessons.

John raised a single eyebrow. "Care to share?"

Teasingly, Alice quipped, "Ah, and what is my incentive to share my deepest, darkest thoughts with you?" She winked a single hunter green eye at him.

John pretended to think for a minute, then snapped his fingers as if he figured out the answer to a particularly difficult question. "Perhaps you would like to share with the man who is currently courting you. After all, I intend to marry you one day."

Alice's face flushed beet red, and she elbowed him in the ribs. "You should have gone with the 'I know all your other secrets.' It probably would have incentivized me more."

"Only probably?" John grinned at her.

Alice shot him a mischievous grin of her own, but before she could respond, a man at the front of the church banged a wooden gavel against the pedestal, calling for silence.

"Ahem," the man cleared his throat. "Thank you, everyone, for gathering here tonight. I am sorry for the dark hour of the meeting."

The Salem witches met during the witch's hour—three in the morning—to avoid detection.

"But as you all know, these are dangerous times for us all. Which brings me to the topic of this meeting. The witch hunts in Europe are growing out of control."

"They've been out of control for years," Giles growled from where he sat with his family and the Parkers. "Goody Glover was hanged in Boston last month. Ever since that blasted manuscript was published two hundred years ago, the humans have used it as an excuse to massacre countless people—humans and witches alike."

A chorus of agreements rang throughout the church, echoing Giles's sentiment.

"It has always been dangerous, but lately, these hunts have ended in massacres that put previous executions to shame," another man argued from the back pews.

"The hunts in Europe are dreadful, absolutely dreadful," a third man spoke from the crowd. "But I do not see how any of this affects us. We are on the other side of the ocean, for Goddess's sake."

"The other side of the ocean?" A woman scoffed. "Since when is Boston located in Europe? The witch hunts are already here, and none of us are safe."

It was the first time a woman spoke, leading the church to descend into madness. The congregation leapt to their feet as they erupted in shouting, screaming at one another from across pews. Neighbors turned on neighbors, and couples and families argued amongst themselves. One woman slapped a man. The shouting grew louder as people fought futilely to make their voices heard over the explosive crowd.

Alice and John sat together in silence.

Hanging her head, Alice rubbed her temples as though she had a headache. Reaching up, John took one of her hands, intertwining his fingers with hers, and kissed the back of her hand. Her eyes snapped to his, and they exchanged a silent conversation in the midst of a raging storm of voices.

I am the Salem Witch, she said. *I should be able to fix this. To stop this chaos.*

You are only fourteen, John reminded her. It was the beginning of September, and she would turn fifteen on the twenty-second. *They will not listen to you unless you tell them who you are. All of who you are.*

Alice gnawed her bottom lip in grave contemplation.

A wooden gavel banged against the podium, though the crowd did not settle until a different, much larger man stepped forward and bellowed, "SILENCE!" His voice echoed through the hall, and every witch in the hall snapped their jaws shut.

"That is better," the man grumbled as he returned to the group of witches standing behind the podium.

"Thank you, George," the man who started the meeting inclined his head. "Now, if you all will give me a minute to explain before jumping to accusations and arguments, we might actually make progress as a community."

The crowd grumbled excuses and apologies as they retook their seats. When everyone was seated, the first man breathed a sigh of relief.

"Now, as I was saying. Whether the witch hunts will make their way to the Salem or not, we cannot be sure, unless one of you has been hiding prophetic abilities."

The man's joke earned several chuckles from the crowd, but Alice's face paled several shades. Frantically, she looked at John. But as he wrapped his arm around her shoulders, she breathed a sigh of relief and sank into his grounding touch.

Alice was not a prophetess, but it was not unusual for the Salem Witch to experience prophetic visions. Nor was it strange for a Nephilim to jump through realms when experiencing dream visions, like the ones that plagued her nightly for the last three weeks.

"We must prepare for the possibility of witch hunts arising here. Let us pray to the Creator that we remain free of this terror, but let us also come to a decision, as a community, on how to address these possibilities."

The room went silent, and Alice's blood rushed through her ears, a pounding sensation thrumming in her head as though it had a heartbeat of its own.

A man stood. "It is simple, is it not? We hide. No magic, ever. No practicing, not even in secret. To enforce this, let us bind our magic. Forever."

"Now hold on there just a minute, Putnam. You cannot make a declaration like that and expect us to dogmatically follow you." Bridget Bishop leapt to her feet, glaring daggers at the man—Putnam. "Last I checked, the Creator gave us free will to make our own individual decisions."

The Coreys had never been fond of Putnam and his family. Neither had the Parkers or most of the town, primarily because of Putnam's greed. He would gladly throw someone under the wagon if it meant getting his way. He had. Literally, he threw a slave in front of a wagon last year. Not to mention his ongoing feud with John Proctor... it was a miracle Proctor wasn't dead yet given how much Putnam despised him.

"Bridget is correct." Giles stood, his chest puffed with pride and unwavering solidarity. "You are asking us to give up part of who we are, and that ain't right."

Several others in the crowd rose to their feet, jumping to Putnam's defense, which spurred others to join the fray and support Giles and Bridget, who was a respected witch, although somewhat of a social outcast among humans.

Relief coursed through Alice at Giles's words. While he and Martha feared detection and dissuaded Alice from using her magic, he was not ready to forfeit his magic altogether. Giles was an air witch, while Martha was a water witch, gifted with healing abilities. As a child, Alice noticed when her mother snuck in a little magic to her herbal remedies or when Alice's injuries mysteriously disappeared overnight. They had never truly forgotten their heritage.

Alice's eyes flicked to Giles, but he was glaring at Putnam. She still had not told her mother and father that she was the Salem Witch, but here they were, siding with her after all these years of hiding their magic.

Magic that Alice was not sure she could hide any longer. Witches had long since cast her sideways glances, their magical senses triggered by the sheer force of the power rolling off her. But Alice could not mute her energy any more than their powers could ignore hers. Even if she could mute her energy, Alice was not sure she wanted to.

Putnam barked back at Giles, then called Bridget an unrepeatable name, earning a collective gasp from the congregation. The witches descended into another useless shouting match.

Closing her eyes, Alice pinched the bridge of her nose.

The man at the podium, the Air Representative of the usually disbanded Athenian Council, banged his gavel repeatedly, but the heavy thumping did not quiet the crowd.

George Jacobs—the General of the disbanded militia of witch Knights—bellowed at the witches, but his deep voice was ineffective to settle the congregation, only adding to the chaos. The other witches behind the podium—the rest of the Athenian Council—screamed at the crowd, trying to silence them, to no avail.

And then the hall went silent.

Alice's eyes flew open as a heavenly presence washed over her. She was paralyzed, unable to move her body except her eyes. The entire congregation was frozen, oblivious to the angel standing inside the church, the top of his golden-bronze locks scraping the support beams of the low ceiling.

Gabriel towered over her, his angel wings lightly scraping the dirt-covered floorboards, but not a speck of dirt marred the pristine white feathers.

"Hello, Alice." Gabriel smiled kindly at her, like a father greeting his daughter. But she was not his child, although she did not know the identity of her father. "Remember, the loudest voice is not always the right one. Fire illuminates the shadows, even in these dark times. Darkness cannot drive out the Darkness. Only Light can do that. This marks the beginning of your Trial of Fire."

He pressed his right hand over her heart, his palm covering less of her body than during her Air Trial since she had grown to stand nearly five-foot-nine, and the other hand covered her forehead.

Purifying white light beamed from his hands, penetrating Alice's mind even as she snapped shut her eyelids. Her eyes stung and her scalp tingled as heavenly magic washed over her, steeping her in the touch of an angel and filling her with the power of Heaven.

Magic burned in her veins, ready to unleash itself on the world. More magic than Alice possessed before, as power was endowed on her from the touch of an angel.

The light faded, and she lurched forward, nearly tumbling out of the pew as the congregation erupted into a frenzy, unaware of what transpired between Alice and Gabriel. Unaware that Alice's long red hair had turned silver and her eyes were now molten pools of metal instead of hunter green. She bore the mark of the Goddess, completely unnoticed by the witches consumed with their argument.

The man at the podium yelled, beseeching the crowd to quell their arguing. "Please, please, people, cease this nonsense. If we do not control our emotions, our energies will attract—"

A thunderous crash sounded from the roof of the church, the wood snapping under the force of the talons slicing through the roof. The claws clenched into fists, then pulled, ripping a gaping hole in the ceiling.

"DEMONS," a woman screeched as witches dove for cover under the pews.

Few witches drew wands, including Giles and Bridget, but even they looked uncertain after so many years of not using their magic.

But Alice did not hesitate.

Surging out of her seat, her silver hair floated on the air currents around her as magic swirled around her entire body. In three swift strides, she reached the altar, directly under the wyvern demon stretching its serpentine neck into the hole, its jaws snapping and leaking saliva.

Alice threw her hand up with a flourish. White holy flames burst from her palm, flying into the demon's open jaws and cooking it from the inside-out. Black dust rained on Alice as she obliterated the demon.

The congregation fell into stunned silence, staring at Alice, but she glared into the open hole in the roof, a vicious scowl marring her beautiful face, making her all the more terrifying with her silver hair and silver orbs glowing with power in place of her eyes.

The witches erupted with a roar of chaos, shouting at Alice, shouting at one another, but Alice ignored them, blasting her magic like a shockwave, sweeping the area for more demons. Her magic returned, slamming into her, and she staggered under the force of what she sensed.

The blood rushed from her face, her skin paling.

Alice whirled on the crowd, magnifying her voice with a simple spell as she pressed the tip of her white oak wand to her throat. "ENOUGH!" she roared, her high-pitched bark sharply silencing the crowd.

"By the Creator..." Bridget Bishop whispered, then dropped to one knee, bowing to show her respect and reverence for the Reigning Salem Witch. The rest of the witches followed her example. Some, like Putnam, were more reluctant than others as they cast murderous glances her way, envious of her apparent power.

But Alice ignored them.

"Rise," Alice commanded, and the witches returned to standing or sat in the pews.

"Goody." When she saved the town from the bobcat during her Air Trial, the townspeople nicknamed her "Goody" for her piety and humanitarian feats. Even so, the man running the meeting stared at her with a mix of horror and awe. "What is the meaning of this?"

John rolled his eyes, then leaned back in his pew, crossing his arms over his chest as he smirked at Alice. "Finally."

Alice smiled sheepishly at him. His parents gawked at him, their glance bouncing between Alice and their son. Giles and Martha merely stared at Alice, their jaws hanging open.

"Enough," Alice repeated, smoothing the front of her simple wool-spun dress. But her eyes were sharp, her senses alert. "There are more," she said softly. "Demons lurk outside these walls, and they *will* attack. It is no longer safe. Prepare yourselves, for we must fight."

As the word left her lips, something rammed against the barricaded doors of the church. Witches shrieked, dropping under the pews, but Alice did not cower as she summoned her elements to her hands.

Air swirled around her left hand in loyalty while green fire licked her palm lovingly. Green. The color of her magic. But the white flames she shot at the demon... white fire was the fire of Heaven. Holy flames.

She was Nephilim, and she would not fall to demons.

John leapt to his feet and rushed to Alice's side, his wand drawn and at the ready as he summoned green magic to his free hand. Like Alice, he had been practicing all these years in secret, discontent to let her carry her burden alone, and while his power could not compare to hers, his magic was strong.

Alice charged for the door, witches leaping from her warpath, and her air sailed ahead of her, blasting the doors open to reveal a pit demon, the guards of the dungeons of Hell. White flames shot from Alice's open palms, engulfing the pit demon, consuming it until it was ash on her wind.

A shivering cold cut through the air as an eerie fog crept from the forest, rolling toward the church.

"What is this?" a woman asked, hugging her arms around her torso. But Alice narrowed her eyes, scanning the forest from where she stood rooted in the doorway of the church.

"It is the middle of July, but the weather is suddenly cold," a man agreed, but Alice did not tear her eyes away from the fog to look for who spoke.

"That ain't cold weather," Thomas Bradbury declared. "That be death approachin'."

They appeared out of nowhere, misshapen figures emerging from the darkness, their fangs repulsively dribbling venom as they breathed out sickly sweet breath.

It was not Death, but it may as well have been.

Demons.

Hundreds of them. Against a congregation of witches who did not have the faintest clue how to use their magic.

Alice's heart dropped into her stomach.

John's hand intertwined with hers, his magic tingling across her skin as though it, too, were trying to reassure her.

But there were so many. And demons of every variety—agony, grave, inferno, brimstone, hellhound, incubi... the list did not end.

A shiver that was not from the cold ran through her.

Demons were born with the powers of Hell within them, so their bodies radiated intense heat. So the cold... where did it come from?

A wrathful sound bellowed from the army of demons.

Bridget Bishop stepped forward, brandishing her wand, but Alice placed a hand on her forearm, stopping her from attacking.

"No, Bridget. This is not a fight you can win."

"But—"

"You may have grown up with magic, but practical magic cannot compare to the power of the elements."

"But—"

Alice cut the older woman off with a look, but John would not let her go so easily.

"Alice, we can fight them off—whatever they are—together. Gather the witches who know how to use their magic and—"

"Please, John," she begged, squeezing his hand. "This is my Trial. No one can help me pass it, and I refuse to lose you."

Sullen, John relinquished his tight grip on her and stepped back, begrudgingly granting her wish.

Stepping out of the light of the church and into the darkness that blanketed the open field, Alice inhaled a deep breath, letting her magic swell within her, amplified by the touch of the angel.

Tonight, she faced the power of Hell.

The only solution was to stand and fight.

Alice called upon her two elements.

Sky above me,

Fire within me.

And then she called upon her mother's element. Earth magic was not yet accessible to her, but as the Nephilim of Earth, nature would always protect her, and she was never separated from the Spirit of the Creator. It would fill her so she may pass this Trial.

Earth below me,
Spirit all around me.

White flames soared from Alice's hands, stretching in a line in front of the church, separating the demons from the witches behind Alice. The hottest fire in all the realms lit the field around Alice, its light throwing the demons' strange shadows against the forest beyond.

Demons could not cross a line of holy flames. And holy flames would burn until the energy was consumed by destroying demons. And with Gabriel's touch transferring angelic power to her, Alice's flames burned brightly with devastating power.

"Alice, let us help you," John called from behind her wall of flames.

"No, John," she said without tearing her eyes away from her enemy. "This is my Trial. I am the Salem Witch, and I will fight until every demon is ash on the wind."

Fire danced in her eyes. Flames were alive in her soul.

Unbridled, burning fury rushed through her veins.

Fire burst to life around Alice, swallowing her like a flame around a wick. Embers burned in her hunter green eyes as an unfathomable power flowed through her body. Rampaging fire licked her body, undulating off her in waves as white holy flames crackled at her fingertips. And she knew, deep in her soul, she could direct the holy fire with a mere thought.

Releasing a resounding roar, the line of demons charged as one, their fangs gnashing and claws slashing as they raced to be the first to sink their talons into her.

Air and fire mingled at her command.

A fierce wind carried white flames, soaring in an arc to blast the front line of demons. They exploded in a storm of ash that rained down on their charging brethren.

The elements were more than individual entities. They worked together to create a formidable force. Fire needed air to live, burning brighter as air stoked the flames. Too much could snuff the flames, but with the anger brewing inside Alice's chest, her fire was greater. Together, fire and air ascended beyond the sum of their parts.

Alice threw white flame after white flame in an unstoppable blaze, the air carrying her heavenly fire as she willed. Not a single shot missed, but the demons did not cease.

Demon after demon rushed at her. Savage brimstone demons, which stood no taller than her waist, charged with their slate-stone horns aimed to gouge out her innards. A lethal blaze poured from her palms, annihilating brimstones by the dozens.

As soon as they were dusted, hellhounds—the feral dogs of Hell— lunged at her. Their hides made them impenetrable to magic, even holy flames. Ducking, Alice rolled under the three hellhounds lunging for her, their jaws snapping.

Another row of hellhounds snapped at the heels of ones she just avoided, and Alice ended up surrounding herself. Growling, the hellhounds' jaws dropped open, revealing the soft, fleshy insides of their mouths.

With a cunning smirk, Alice summoned her magic. Arrows made of flames shot from her fingertips at the hellhounds, soaring through their dripping fangs to pierce their vulnerable throats from the inside. Nothing but dust remained of the demented dogs, but Alice found herself encircled by half a dozen agony demons, powerful lesser demons that were known as the most brutal fighters of the underworld, but their eyes were their weak spots.

Eight feet tall and ugly, agony demons were the demons of nightmares. Red hellfire burned along the agony demons' curled goat horns and down their necks, over flesh burnt to the sinewy muscle, and three rows of vicious teeth grinned from within their jaws. Agony demons were nearly impossible to kill without a weapon, and Alice only had holy flames and the sharp wit of her mind.

The agony demons attacked as though they shared one mind. But Alice was not an unintelligent demon. She was the Salem Witch, and the Salem Witch had *two* elements at her command. Not just one.

Alice summoned a wind to throw her into the air. Spinning over their heads, her silver locks snapped on the currents and her dress skirts tangled around her legs. As she descended, Alice hit one of the demons in the back with a spray of holy flames.

It flew forward, smacking into the agony demon across from it. But Alice's magic did not kill the demon, and as she expelled her magic, her holy flames weakened.

The agony demon closest to her lunged, slashing at her with its claws. She met it with a stream of white flames.

Even if she killed these agony demons, more awaited their turn to attack her. She needed a weapon or a sword. The tiny, dull two-inch long, knife that she hid in her shoe would be useless against this demonic army. There were just too many. She needed something larger, something she could use to pierce their eyes, which was easiest way to kill the beasts.

Her gaze landed on the curled horns of the agony demon closest to her, and her mouth curved into a smile.

Summoning flames to her hands once more, feeling the drain on the magic in her gut, Alice fashioned the flames into a flat disc. Before the creatures could attack, she launched the disc through the air, controlling its trajectory with her mind and magic.

The disc of fire sank into the agony demon's horn, not too close to the base where the horn was thickest but not too close to the tip that she could not hold the horn. Her fire sank halfway through the horn before the magic was consumed.

Alice palmed another fiery disc, but the agony demons charged. She threw it, letting it fly past the moving demon, then threw herself out of the way, rolling across the uneven earth before popping to her feet, while letting her magic control the white disc of flames.

Bouncing back like a boomerang, the fiery disc soared through the air to cut into the demon's partially cut horn, severing it from the rest of its head.

Throwing its head back, the demon howled in pain, but Alice scooped up the horn. And as she rose on a whirlwind of air, she shoved the tip of the horn through the hellfire eyes of the agony demon, dooming it to dust.

Dropping to the ground, Alice spun and ducked under the swipe of an arm from another agony demon, then threw the horn, directing it with air magic to pierce another's eye. The horn returned to her hand with a thought, and she dodged the demon.

Wielding magic like the witch she was born to be, Alice used her make-shift weapon like a warrior, felling the remaining agony demons with her unexpected combat prowess.

Dropping the horn, Alice turned to face the next group of attacking demons, fire dancing along her skin. Summoning holy flames was a magically consuming feat, and Alice's heart thundered in her chest from a mix of the exertion and adrenaline.

But the demons were falling back, dying beneath Alice's onslaught. She was a one-woman army, decimating demons with her menacing air and frantic fire magic and leaving nothing but ash blowing in the wind.

Charging forward, Alice screamed an infernal scream and unleashed a torrent of lethal flames from her hands at the fleeing demons. She refused to allow even one to escape.

Holy flames spread in a circle, wrapping around the clearing behind the church, trapping the demons in with her. The fleeing demons skidded to a halt, then turned to face her as fear danced across their faces.

They had attacked her under the mistaken impression that, together, they could overwhelm her. Foolish demons.

Weaponless, Alice channeled the only weapon she had, the weapon she was born with—her magic—and for the first time in her life, she felt like a witch. A witch with unrivaled magic.

The army of darkness dwindled as she shot flame after flame, air magic directing the fire to always hit her mark. Whips of fire extended from Alice's hands, and she snapped them like a conductor leading an orchestra. The flames cracked across the bodies of demons, drawing black blood from the slashes she tore in their skin. A second hit killed the weaker demons. And a third killed more, until only a handful of wrath-filled demons remained.

Five demons charged her at once.

Sucking the fire whips into her palms, Alice redirected her magic as the first demon descended on her.

Her flat palm hit the brimstone demon square in the chest, burning her hand print into its slate-stone skin. It screamed in pain, but Alice silenced it by driving her hand deeper into its chest cavity and ripping out its black heart.

The demon exploded into dust, but the heart pumped its final beats in Alice's hand.

She threw it at the second demon, hitting it in the head. It was an agony demon. Rising on a mini whirlwind, Alice stood face to face with the demon as she plunged her flame-laced fingers into its eye sockets, gouging out its vulnerable flesh. Dust rained to the ground.

The third and fourth demons reached her at the same time. But Alice merely raised a hand, her palm facing down, and slammed it toward the ground. A gust of air slammed into the demons from above, pinning them to the ground. Fire leapt from her hands, incinerating the demons in a flash of green and white.

The last demon, a purgatory demon, charged at her.

Inhaling a steady breath, Alice summoned the diminishing power in her core and brought her flames to life. Launching a ball of green fire at the demon, Alice simultaneously raised herself on the wind, flipping over the demon's head while it dodged her fireball.

Landing lightly on her feet behind the demon, she watched as it halted its warpath, its head moving back and forth as it searched for her. Demons were not the brightest beings… how could they be when they were created by the dark acts of the Mother of Demons instead of by the Light of the Creator?

Reaching down, Alice removed the small knife she kept strapped inside her latchet shoe. It would have been useless against an army of demons, but a lone purgatory demon, which must be killed with holy flames or a knife to its black heart, would be fun to kill this way.

Green flames edged the simple blade, measuring no more than two inches long. Alice ran at it from behind, and leaping into the air, she slammed against its back. Her stature was not enough to topple it, so she wrapped one arm around its meaty neck in a chokehold and raised the hand holding the knife, then plunged the tiny blade into the purgatory demon's chest. A sickening squelch sounded as the demon gasped out a breath, its body slackening under Alice.

Releasing the demon, Alice let its body fall to the ground where its decaying husk deteriorated into dust.

As Alice slayed the last demon, resolve settled within her soul. She would master her magic, with or without the support of Salem. And a strange tug in her gut told her it would be the death of her.

Magic rushed through her with alarm, screaming out as it detected the threat nearby. Alice's head snapped up, forgetting the pile of ash at her feet as her eyes scanned her wall of holy flames circling the field.

Darkness swelled from the forest, an entity made of inky shadows emerging from the blackness of the trees. Flying over her wall of holy flames, the dark entity crossed without harm.

Alice staggered back a step. How did it cross the flames?

CHAPTER FOUR

NIGHTMARES AND WEDDINGS

The earth sang to Alice, her mother's domain speaking to her out of loyalty. This entity did not care about the witches. It was coming for her, and it was *evil*. A dark being. But worse, it was powerful. Possibly more powerful than the Nephilim-Salem Witch.

The undulating mass of black shadows surged toward her.

Alice did not think, she did not breathe as her power rose within her to seize her entire body. The shadow creature was nearly upon her, and then it disappeared, replaced by the trees of the forest.

No, *Alice* had disappeared. She whirled around. The dark entity hovered over the ground near her wall of holy flames that protected the congregation of witches.

She *spooked*.

A rare ability only the extremely powerful could perform, and Alice had done it. She disappeared, moved through space, and re-materialized somewhere new.

Alice raised a hand filled with white flames, curling it into a fist. "Come and get it," she snarled at her dark enemy.

Releasing a guttural roar, the demonic entity rushed her, flying through the air faster than a human eye could track. But Alice was no human.

She spooked, reappearing behind the demon.

Vibrant green and while flames soared from her open palms in a fiery stream, blasting into the back of the demon.

It released a blood-curdling shriek and slammed into the ground. Alice realized with a start... it may have been comprised of shadows, but it was a tangible being. More tangible than the air blowing through Alice's fingers.

And if it was tangible, Alice could hurt it.

Green flames sparked to life in her hair, crowning her head like a queen reigning over her kingdom.

Stretching her hands out to the side, she summoned the white holy flames that encircled the field behind the church into her palms, consuming the power of the fire to replenish her depleted energy stores. She needed all of her magic to combat this evil.

The dark entity rushed her again. Fire unleashed from her hands, but the Darkness flew through her flames. In a flash of dark green light, Alice spooked, barely avoiding the dark entity before it rammed into her.

Spheres of fire sprang into her cupped palms.

Throwing a ball of flames at the Darkness, she allowed her air magic to take control, directing her flames to strike her assailant. Then she threw the next, and the next, each time summoning another sphere of fire after she threw one.

Each time her fireball struck, the Darkness paused as it absorbed her attack, unphased for but a moment. But she was not hurting it. Merely stalling its inevitable assault. Even so, she threw another ball of fire. Then another, until the Darkness was upon her.

Green light wrapped around her, and Alice re-materialized on the other end of the field, away from the church housing the congregation of witches. Breathing heavily, she faced the Darkness, summoning smaller spheres of fire to her hands.

Mere fireballs would not defeat it, even if they were composed of holy flames. Her magic caused minimal damage, and she could not sustain the flow of power for much longer.

Again, the Darkness attacked, but Alice did not draw upon her magic just yet, letting the Darkness approach in a blur. Hitting the ground, Alice dodged under the Darkness, then rolled so she was face up with the Darkness hovering above her.

Dark tentacles stretched for her. Alice shoved her flaming hands into the center of the undulating mass.

Fire flew from her open palms, searing the underside of the Darkness. Shrieking, it pulled away, fleeing.

Shooting to her feet, Alice did not dare take her eyes off her opponent. She could not beat it head on. But when her hands were inside it...

Alice knew how to defeat it... if only temporarily.

Throwing fireball after fireball, Alice lulled it into a false sense of security, allowing it to think she was unaware of the impact her heavenly fire inflicted from within the Darkness, as though it burned it from the inside out.

Because a strange tug in her gut told her that the Darkness wanted to devour her, to consume her power, and the only way it could do that was by surrounding her and stealing her life force, but in doing so, it made itself vulnerable to her.

Pretending to tire from the exertion, which was not hard to do as her magic reserves dwindled to the dredges, Alice shot smaller fireballs at the Darkness. Her attacks were hardly effective.

Stopping altogether, she bent and the waist and braced her hands on her knees, giving the Darkness the opportunity it so desired. And the one she needed.

It rushed her.

Alice stumbled back as though she were trying to escape, but the Darkness was fast, faster than her, and in a blink of an eye, all she saw was indigo as the Darkness swarmed her, and Alice nearly lost herself in it.

Its acrid stench—rot and mildew, mold and decay—shoved up her nostrils, and she choked as the entity overwhelmed her senses. It sought to devour her. Her identity. Her memories. Her magic. And she forgot herself. Who was she again? Her name... what was her name?

"Alice!" John screamed, but it was distant, as though he were shouting through water. But his voice...

White flames erupted from Alice like a volcano spewing lava. Fire burned around her body, turning her into a pillar of biblical flames, and the Darkness shrieked, cringing away from her.

But she was *inside* the Darkness, surrounded by it.

Fire raged around her like a bonfire, searing the inside of the dark entity as the flames engulfed it in a lake of fire. Even dousing the Darkness in heavenly flames was not enough to kill it.

Hissing, it reared back, pulling away from Alice, but she pushed her magic farther, letting her holy flames leap at the Darkness in an offensive assault.

The indigo mass of darkness undulated, twisting to avoid her flames, but Alice was determined to pummel this dark being such that it knew the extent of her power and feared it, knowing the Darkness could never overcome her light.

Stretching out a hand, she wrapped her fingers around an indigo tendril of the dark entity, seizing hold of the Darkness. White fire burned in her palm, searing the Darkness until it screamed, yanking its tendril back to escape Alice's grasp.

But she held it with a ferocious grip, wrapping her other hand around the Darkness, flames sparking at her fingertips. Shoving her hand at the Darkness, a powerful blast of holy flames exploded from her palms in a fiery torrent, plowing into the serpentine dark entity. Fire poured from her in an unrelenting display of heavenly magic.

Shrieking, the Darkness wrenched free of Alice's grasp, but she did not cease her assault. Channeling more power, Alice increased the force of the flames flowing from her hands.

The Darkness flew away from her, heading toward the tree line.

It was going to escape.

Alice gathered a ball of white fire in her hand, yanked it back and launched it forward, letting her air magic carry the fire faster than the wind until it slammed into the dark entity, searing the Darkness after Alice's cunning attack weakened it.

With an agonized shriek, the Darkness plunged into the dark forest, leaving Alice standing alone in the field outside the church, the other witches watching in fearful, awed silence.

Her chest heaving from the exertion of fighting with magic, Alice breathed in the humid air, warm now that the Darkness had fled. Staring at the line of dark trees, Alice realized she was not the person she had been mere minutes ago. She had been forged anew in the heat of the holy flames she summoned.

Something sparked within her, a fire unlike any fire that burned on earth. This one was green and all-consuming. It was the fire that would burn brightly within her until she left this mortal plane. And she would only do so after fighting vehemently against this evil.

Because Alice knew without a doubt, the Darkness she encountered was the evil tainting the land, corrupting mortals, and before her Salem War was over, either her or it would be dead.

She could no longer afford to hope for someone to help her. Alice must help herself, and she fully accepted the responsibility entrusted to her by Heaven.

Covered in black blood and demon dust, Alice spun on her heel and stomped to the church, through the double wide doors, and marched to the dais of the church, stopping before the altar, then spun to face the congregation of witches.

Fury radiated off her as green flames sparked to life in her silver hair. Her eyes glowed brighter than the moon, with the power of Heaven shining from her irises.

"Witches of Salem," Alice addressed the gathered witches. "You know me as Alice Corey, daughter of Giles and Martha, and yes, this is true. But you have speculated the legitimacy of this claim, for you do not know the identity of my birth mother." The crowd stared at her expectantly with bated breath, the silence weighing heavily on her shoulders. Alice's hunter green eyes met John's matching gaze. With an encouraging smile, John nodded for her to continue. With a deep breath, she announced, "I am the daughter of Uriel, the Archangel of Earth."

Jaws dropped as witches stared at her in a mix of wonder and rage. Witches dropped to their knees, bowing to her. Others shouted at her and argued amongst themselves, but most sat in stunned silence.

Simply raising her hand, Alice silenced the hall once more.

"I know you have questions, but please, let me finish what I have to say." She inhaled a deep breath, then launched into her speech. "None of us were alive the last time a Salem Witch was chosen, but we all know what it means—a Salem War is coming. And it is coming for us all. I am the Salem Witch, and I will do everything within my power to protect you. I do not know what war will bring. All I know is Heaven chose me to lead you.

"But for the first time, I am choosing to be your leader. I will follow the path that Heaven has set before me. I will master the elements, and I will end this war, but I need you, all of you, to help me. Hiding our magic is *not* the solution. It has not saved the men and women from being slaughtered in the Old World. They are humans and witches alike, persecuted out of fear. We can run from this war, but eventually, it will catch up to us. Instead, we must be prepared to fight, and to fight with any means we have. To fight with our *magic.* I have used my magic every day since Gabriel declared me the Salem Witch when I was ten, and I have yet to be discovered, so it *can* be done."

Putnam, who advocated binding their magic earlier, rose to his feet. "What if we do not want to use our magic?"

"Anyone who does not wish to use their magic will not be forced to do so." Alice curled her hand into a fist as a symbol of strength and solidarity in front of her fellow witches. "However, if you wish to fully embrace everything you are, then you are free to make that choice. Do not let anybody else make your choices for you, not even me. I only ask you to use magic carefully to avoid discovery."

Putnam breathed a sigh of relief and nodded to Alice. "Thank you."

"When do we start training?" Bridget grinned wickedly at Alice, then winked. "Daughter of Uriel?"

Alice's lips slowly twisted into a smile. "Go home, rest. Those of you who wish to train, we will gather at Misery Islands Cove tomorrow at sundown. I will teach you to use your magic."

In a flash of white, Gabriel materialized in front of the congregation. There was a collective intake of air, and then every witch dropped to one knee before the angel, clasping their right fist over their hearts.

Gabriel rumbled to the congregation, "Rise." His ocean blue eyes landed on Alice, a warm smile stretching his lips. "Reaching harmony within and accepting all of who you are is the essence of the Trial of Fire. You had to accept your role as the Salem Witch, as the leader and protector of your people, if you are to win this war. Darkness grows stronger in Salem, but if you remain rooted in who you are, you will always be able to summon the light of Heaven. Congratulations, Alice. You have passed your Trial of Fire."

Pressing one hand to her heart and the other to her forehead, white light yielded from Gabriel's hands, penetrating Alice's very soul. The power of Heaven crashed through her, obliterating the wall separating her from the rest of her magic.

Her water magic.

The element washed over her with the force of a waterfall, its magic pumping through her veins like a raging sea.

Alice gasped as her power unleashed itself, whipping across the church like a shockwave before she pulled the magic into her body to swirl in her core.

Alice's hair returned to its vibrant red hue, and her eyes glittered their usual hunter green. Every witch in Salem witnessed Alice Urielson Corey pass her Fire Trial.

And as one, they clapped a fist over their hearts and sank to one knee, bowing to the daughter of Uriel, the Salem Witch who would save them from the Darkness that sought to destroy them.

Standing at the water's edge, Alice's water magic danced among the waves lapping at the shore.

In an hour, she was to be Mrs. John Parker. And as such, she would move into the little house off the Salem Harbor Waterfront that John rented from Mary English, a fellow witch. She was to be *married.*

Her heart soared at the thought. All these years together, learning magic together, facing her Trials with him by her side, and they were finally to be married.

She only wished... no, she would not let the thought taint the occasion.

John was hers, and she was his, and that was all that mattered. And her magic sang, fueled by the joy filling her heart. Inhaling in a deep breath, Alice let her magic wander freely, sensing every molecule of water as it moved with the power of the ocean.

Alice was like the ocean. Powerful, yet calm, but when enraged, she could drown the strongest of men.

By the Creator, she was lucky John wanted to marry her, else she would never find a husband. Strong women were not usually lucky enough to find strong, agreeable men like John.

It was 1690, and Alice was unlike other women. Despite the town calling her Goody, she was not pious and quiet and polite. She was stubborn and bull-headed like any true earth witch, but those were not exactly qualities becoming of a woman, especially during these times. Alice wondered if her mother, Uriel, had such a bold personality.

Make no mistake, Little Bull, your steadfastness comes from me as surely as your bull-headedness. The Archangel Uriel's voice filled Alice's head, and she smiled to herself that her mother was listening to her thoughts. *Although I cannot be physically present with you on this special day, know that I am watching over you.*

"Are you ready, Alice?" Giles asked from behind her. He did not startle her, for Alice's magic sensed him from afar.

Beaming, she turned her back on the ocean to take her father's offered elbow.

"More than I have been ready for anything else in my life."

With a faint smile, Giles led Alice down the path the wound through the forest, away from the ocean and her water magic, until they reached the doors of the Church of Salem.

Nodding to the ushers, Alice sucked in a deep breath.

This was it.

The doors widened, opening slowly, and the humans and witches gathered inside the church for Alice's wedding rose as one body to face her and Giles.

Music sounded from the organ at the front, and on cue, Giles led his daughter forward, walking her down the aisle. Tears of joy sprung to Alice's eyes as she watched her future husband, unable to look away as he wiped his own hunter green eyes.

Not soon enough, Alice arrived at the altar where her father handed her off to John with a kiss on the cheek, but Alice only had eyes for her betrothed.

The ceremony passed in a blur, but Alice could not recall a single detail other than John. The feel of his hands on hers, the sound of his voice as he swore his vows, the look in his eyes as he stared into hers. Her soul was consumed by him.

"Until death do us part." John leaned in to whisper, "And even after that, my soul will always find you."

The next words to leave Alice's mouth were, "I do."

"You may kiss the bride."

Alice barely heard the priest as John leaned in, capturing her mouth with his, and a cheering applause rang through the tiny church.

She was his and he was hers, in sickness and in health, through the good times and the bad.

And through the Salem Witch Trials.

Alice floated in the water, deep under the sea, so far beneath the surface that no light could penetrate the inky indigo waters.

Spinning, Alice turned through the water, the pressure slowing her movements. Darkness invaded her senses, but she could draw breath. After all, water was her current element.

But why was she here? At the bottom of the ocean?

Glancing down, she gasped in a breath, choking at the sight. A ship lay wrecked on the ocean floor, its mass and booms ripped free and discarded elsewhere. The hull of the ship was shredded to pieces, the wood torn from the side, leaving a gaping hole open to the cabin under the deck.

Sharks swarmed the waters, circling the ship as blood blossomed from the wreckage. Alice swam forward, nearing the ship, but the sharks ignored her in their hunt for fresh blood.

Blood that floated away from the bodies of the crew that lay dead with the ship.

"No," Alice spoke, the word bubbling out of her mouth, the sound muted by the water. Shaking her head, she spun to leave, to swim far, far away from the wreckage, then stopped.

"John?" she asked with a gasp. Her husband stood before her, as unaffected by the water as her. His mouth moved, opening and closing as though he were speaking, but no words came out.

Tears welled in her eyes to be washed away with the salt water as she reached for him. Stretching out a hand, he made to grab hold of her.

From behind him rose an inky, undulating indigo mass, its tentacles stretching for them.

"John," Alice screamed his name, grasping at him, but the water resisted her. Alice thrashed her limbs violently in a futile attempt to swim toward him, her fingers mere inches from his. She tried to summon her magic, to make the element bend to her will, but nothing answered. She did not feel the element calling to her as it should. "John!"

A heartbreaking scream tore from her throat as the Darkness seized hold of her husband, the inky tendrils slithering around him like serpents until he was gone, stolen right in front of her.

"No!"

Alice shot up in bed, a layer of sweat coating her entire body as she gasped in deep breaths. Burying her face in her hands, Alice wept, her entire body shaking.

"Alice?" John asked groggily as he sat up, rubbing at his bleary eyes. "Alice, what is wrong?" His warm arms wrapped around her, pulling her to his chest.

"John," she said his name between sobs. "John, I-I-I saw you d-die. My d-d-dream... you were t-t-taken from my arms. I-I could not... could not save you."

"Shh, shh." John stroked her fiery red hair back from where it stuck to the sweat on her face. "Do not fret, dear Wife. I will never leave you."

"You do not know that." Alice shook harder as she swallowed her sobs. "You died at sea, John. Your ship wrecked. The ocean... it was angry. I could feel Her rage, and She unleashed Her wrath on your ship."

"It is okay, Alice. It was just a dream."

"You do not know that," she repeated, knowing it was more than a dream.

He did not understand. How could he? He was not the Salem Witch nor a Nephilim nor a prophet. Never had he experienced the visions Alice endured because of her magic. Her dreams were not normal dreams, but dream visions sent to her from the angels, a message heralding a warning.

"It was a vision, John, from the angels."

"You do not know that, and there is no sense in worrying about what may or may not come to pass. We have each other right now. Let us cherish the present. Come back to bed and let me hold you while you sleep."

Intuition rolled through her stomach. It was no mere dream.

"I see darkness where you see light," Alice muttered.

How could her husband be so optimistic? How could he ignore the fear that threatened to swallow her whole at the thought of losing him?

Raising a hand to her cheek, he cupped her face with his palm, drawing her eyes up to his matching green ones. "Listen to me, Alice. Nothing can separate me from you. All the forces of Darkness could attack, and I know you would fight your way through hell to find me, as I would do for you. I will always find you, in this life and the next. My heart and soul will always belong to you."

Wrapping an arm around her, he gently pulled her to the soft bedding, then pulled the covers up to wrap their bodies in warmth.

But the warmth of John's body did little against the paralyzing cold that had seized Alice, seeping into her bones.

"All will be well, Alice," John whispered into her ear as he pulled her back flush against his chest.

A single tear rolled down her cheek to soak into the pillow.

"No, it will not," she prophesized grimly.

CHAPTER FIVE

THE STORM

Bridget Bishop was a force to be reckoned with.

The Bishop family possessed powerful magical abilities, dating back to the invention of the written word. They were some of the first witches in recorded history and had been present in every Salem War and survived. And Bridget Bishop was no exception. She fought with a ferocity that rivaled Alice's own unyielding nature.

And she never missed a practice, attending nightly to the dark and desolate Misery Islands no matter the weather to train with the Salem Witch.

As a water witch, Bridget had plenty of her element to practice with while surrounded by the ocean on the island, and her and Alice often split from the main practice group to spar with the element, exchanging blows and strikes, and learning new skills together.

It was as much a benefit to Alice as it was to Bridget. For once, the Salem Witch had a companion to train with, and she found herself progressing quicker than she had with either of her previous elements.

Of course, many of the witches elected to *not* practice their craft, but younger witches, like Benjamin Nurse, eagerly joined Alice on the Misery Islands. Bridget was among the few adults, including Alice's parents, Giles and Martha, and John's parents, the Parkers. Fear still gripped the hearts of many. But some were better than none. Alice did not know what her Salem War held, but it was widely known that no witch could escape unscathed.

Except the cowards fleeing Salem.

Once Alice ousted herself as the Salem Witch, many families fled, fearing the certain doom they expected to befall Salem. Perhaps they were right, but Alice could not, and would not, run.

As Alice faced off against Bridget, the other witches gathered around them. John watched the ferocious women closely, his arms crossed over his chest.

Winking at John, Alice twirled her wrist, snapping a whip of water at Bridget, who ducked and rolled under the attack. Popping to her feet, Bridget brandished her wand, calling the water from the ocean to surge into a wave. The swell rushed at Alice to crush her under a waterfall of pressure.

Alice raised a hand, parting the water to either side of her. Grabbing hold of the element, Alice let it hover around her, then froze it into daggers of ice. She launched dagger after dagger, forcing Bridget to duck and spin and dodge and parry, until at last, Bridget grabbed hold of one of the daggers, spun around, and threw it at Alice.

The attack was not overwhelming, but enough to distract Alice so Bridget could melt her remaining daggers. A stream of water flew at Alice from Bridget's wand. Hitting the ground, Alice rolled under the water, then popped to her feet and deflected the water with the palm of her hand.

And on and on, the two women fought with nothing but their magic as they steadily closed the gap separating them. They danced across the clearing, to and fro, sideways, backwards, and forwards, as the other witches watched with scrutiny.

If Alice used all three elements, Bridget would be no match for her, but sparring with a single element challenged Alice to improve her skills with water magic in the face of Bridget's calm ferocity.

Alice stepped forward as water burst from her palms, hitting Bridget in the chest. Bridget's back smacked the tense surface of the ocean, knocking the wind from her lungs, but she splashed to her feet, her wool dress soaked through.

Approaching the edge where land met the sea, Alice raised her hands to block the attack Bridget launched at her. Water sliced toward her, and Alice diverted the magic, then shot her own attack, which Bridget also deflected.

The witches exchanged strike after strike until sweat beaded on their foreheads from the exertion of fighting despite the chilled night air.

And then Bridget pulled a crafty maneuver. Snapping a water whip at Alice, Bridget simultaneously commanded the water at Alice's feet to surge up, splashing her in the face. Rearing back, Alice blinked away the sting of salt water, her vision blurry.

A torrent of water slammed into her, throwing her until she rolled to a stop in the sand. As she struggled to her hands and knees, a swell crashed down on Alice and smacked her into the sand again.

Bridget cackled with maniacal laughter from where she stood in the water as she smashed another wave against the Salem Witch.

A sly grin claimed Alice's lips.

Slapping a hand against the wet sand, her green magic shot toward the ocean, freezing the water it passed over. As it rushed for Bridget, Alice's magic spread far and wide, freezing every molecule of water in the bay surrounding the island.

Bridget's eyes widened in surprise, but it was too late. She could not escape the frozen tundra that slammed into her, freezing her legs in the ocean, then creeping up her torso to freeze her soaked garments. Even her arm sleeves solidified into blocks of ice, and Bridget could no longer move, meaning she could no longer command the element.

Powerful as the Bishop family was, Alice was the only witch with the power to telepathically conduct the elements according to her will.

Rising to full height, Alice smirked at her friend frozen in a block of ice. Bridget glowered at her, then threw her head back and cackled.

"Release me, would you? So we may spar another round."

It was Alice's turn to chuckle as she swiped a hand through the air, melting the bay instantly. "Are you sure you want to face my might again? You may find yourself trapped in an iceberg."

Trudging through the water, Bridget swiped her wand over her body, pulling the water off her clothes. "Mind summoning a fire before I freeze to death?"

Snapping her fingers, Alice summoned green flames to the pit at the edge of the clearing and led Bridget to stand beside it while the women spoke.

John approached Alice from behind, wrapping his arms around her and drawing her into his chest. His warmth surrounded her, as did his earthy scent, and Alice breathed in deeply.

"That was rather impressive," he murmured into her hair, distracting her from the conversation she held with Bridget. "It will not be long until you master this element, too, and then you and I can spar."

"Careful what you ask for, boy," Bridget warned. "This woman will pummel you without remorse, whether you are courting her or not."

Alice grinned at the older woman. While years separated Alice and Bridget, she felt a certain kinship with the Bishop woman. They held the same beliefs regarding magic and witching world politics, and Bridget trained with as much gusto as the Salem Witch herself. Bridget, who had years of magical experience before it was outlawed, willingly shared her knowledge with Alice, intent on strengthening the Salem Witch more than she cared for her own success. Bridget was the closest thing to a mentor Alice ever had.

"Then perhaps all of us lesser witches should spar against Alice together—give her a challenge for once."

Frowning, Bridget stared at the other witches as they drilled the basic techniques of elemental magic.

Alice shared Bridget's mind.

The other witches were not ready. Even the older witches, who had trained decades ago, were not adept enough to face Alice. After this break, she would have to return to assisting them in their training, teaching new techniques and correcting old ones. She cringed at the sloppy mistakes she witnessed on the training field.

Fear twanged in her chest. If they could not defeat the Salem Witch together, then how were they to survive the war to come against demons led by the dark entity Alice faced in her Trial of Fire?

And for the first time, Alice realized that all of Salem would perish if she could not overcome the Darkness.

John hoisted his satchel on his shoulder as he strode down the wooden pier toward the plank of the ship. John was running from yet another uncomfortable conversation with his wife.

Like the other sailors, he was eager to return to work after the cold months. It was early March, and winter had thawed enough for the crew to set sail and transport cargo on behalf of the merchants.

Alice marched after him with silver eyes and hair. She had been stuck in the middle of her Water Trial for three weeks, ever since John announced he was hitting the high seas on a voyage to the Old World.

All this magic coursing through her veins, amplified by the Archangel Gabriel's touch, yet she was powerless to stop her husband from boarding that wretched ship.

Nobody blinked an eye at her silver features because of the glamour she cast over her face, making her hair appear as its normal fiery red and her eyes the hunter green she inherited from Uriel.

"John," her voice was steel as she said his name. "Do not dare walk away from me in the middle of a conversation."

He released a haggard sigh before turning to her. "Alice," he pleaded, "we have had this conversation a hundred times. I am going. End of story."

"Not end of story," she growled at him, her hands curling into fists. "We need to discuss this further."

"What is there to discuss?" John demanded. "You have a bad feeling. What am I supposed to do? Not go?"

"Yes," she practically roared. Her face slipped from its stony mask as deep-seated worry stole her features.

"I cannot shirk my responsibilities simply because of a feeling, Alice. If I renege my word, I will sully my reputation, and then how will I find work?"

"You are not a water elemental, John. You belong with both feet on the ground, touching the earth. It is unnatural for an earth witch to spend so much time away from his element." Her voice turned pleading. "John, it is not just this feeling. I... you know about the dream visions."

She visibly shivered, rubbing her hands along her goose fleshed arms. As messages from their celestial parents, dream visions were unique to Nephilim, with the exception of the Salem Witch, who received visions from the Messenger Archangel on behalf of the Goddess who marked Alice as Her own.

"Bad dreams of what is to happen. It is the same vision every night. You board this ship and sail away, smiling and waving at me as the sun shines on us. And then the dream is swallowed by darkness. Only it is not just dark. It is the Ocean, and She is angry. The water, normally a beautiful aquamarine, turns navy as darkness seeps in. Then you are standing before me, talking, but I cannot hear you. Your face turns frantic, and you reach for me, but when I reach out to grab you, your fingers slip through mine, and you fall into the raging ocean and are swallowed by the waves, lost to the storm."

Alice was shaking by the time she finished recounting her dream. John pulled her into his chest, wrapping his arms around her and rubbing his hand along her spine, whispering soothing nothings into her ear.

"I-I c-cannot l-lose you, John," Alice stuttered.

"Shh, shh. I know, and you will not lose me. If I die, I will reincarnate a hundred times until I make my way back to you. My soul only has one love. Only you, my Alice."

Choking on a sob, she managed to speak through the emotion. "It is just... these visions or dreams or whatever they are, they feel like premonitions." She lifted her head off his chest, raising a hand to John's cheek. "You are my everything, John. This year has been hard enough, and with my birthday..." As she trailed off, understanding and worry crept into John's face. He knew the direness of Alice circumstances. Circumstances he could do nothing to change.

"Oh, my sweet Alice. Nothing could stand in the way of you and your Trial. I have complete faith you will pass with flying colors. You are the toughest woman I know, and the strongest witch I will ever meet. I will only be a hindrance as you train. A distraction. And this is my livelihood. We need the money. This is for the best." He sighed deeply. "You need to focus on your Trials, not on starting a family with me. My presence, my wants, are not helping that."

Fresh waves of tears streamed down Alice's cheeks as she touched her forehead to John's. What about her wants? Did her desire for a family not matter? Did the angels not consider that when Heaven selected her to fight this war? If she died in this war, Uriel's bloodline would end with her, and she had no children to carry on her legacy. No children to leave with John, so he might always have a piece of her. As though he were thinking the same thing, a tear fell from his eye, plopping against the wooden planks of the dock.

"When you return..." She choked on a sob, then swallowed thickly, burying her face in his chest. "When you return, I will have passed my Trials and ended this Salem War. Then we will start our family. Together. As our Creator intended."

"Try to stop me." He smiled before his lips claimed hers in a breath-stealing goodbye kiss.

"I love you," he whispered to her. "More than Eden itself."

"And I love you," she said, her voice hoarse as she strained to speak through the emotion. "More than Earth itself."

Too soon, he pulled away, and with one last pained glance, he walked down the planks to join the other men preparing the boat for passage across the ocean.

All the while, Alice stood on the deck, staring at the massive ship as the sails were hoisted, ropes were thrown and wrangled, and cargo was loaded.

An hour later, the ship and crew were ready to shove off. Oars extended from the slots in the sides of the ship, the crew ready to begin at the captain's command. John appeared at the side of the ship, leaning against the rail as his eyes found Alice's. The emotion that passed between them with just a look spoke volumes of their love.

With a strange mix of excitement and dismay, John raised his hand in farewell. Tears streaming down her cheeks, Alice copied his movement, but instead of dropping her hand, she raised it straight in the air. As her palm opened above her head, a mighty gust of wind caught the sails, propelling the ship through the water and pushing it out to sea.

The magic of her first element sailed through her open fingers, the air a tangible element to her touch. With the power of an angel's touch magnifying her magic, the squall raged through the skies above, filling the ship's sails until they strained against their tethers.

Alice's magic tore out of her again, this time diving into the ocean currents below the wharf. She could sense the essence of the water, how it moved and flowed, how it supported the weight of the ship. And she parted the sea. Not like Moses, but enough for the ship to cut through the waves at a clipped pace as she pushed it from behind with the powers of sky and sea.

Other wives and children of the crew gathered on the wharf around Alice to send off the ship, waving, shouting, and cheering as the ship cut through the water, headed for the open ocean. But as the ship shrank, sailing toward the horizon, the cheering diminished, and the families departed.

Except Alice, who stood on those wooden planks, unmoving until the ship sank into the horizon, too far for the human eye to see, even with magic.

Alice dropped her head, her hands folding together. Her lips moved silently, her words a prayer unheard by anyone except the wind and Heaven. Finishing her prayer to the Creator, she lifted her head and looked to the horizon one last time before turning her back to the ocean, the element whose Trial she was stuck in.

"Do not fret, we shall see them again," another wife said from beside Alice. Martha Dutch—a human.

Emotion choked Alice, and for a moment, she forgot herself as she said, "No. Our husbands shall never return home." And with that dismal declaration, she turned on her heel and left the other wife alone on the wharf.

Disheartened, she slowly made the cold, lonely trek to the house she used to share with her husband. Pushing through the worn wooden door, she entered the simple house, and a shadow of dread fell upon her. With exaggerated slowness, as though she were moving through water, she prepared dinner, and meandered around the house, performing random chores, trying to occupy her mind so she did not dwell on the man missing from her side or the silver pigment of her hair reminding her of her Water Trial.

With a wave of her hand, green flames sparked to life in the hearth, her second element answering her call. As she twisted her wrist, her magic playing with the flames, a coy smile formed on her lips as she reveled in the warmth of the fire and the pleasant burn of the magic flooding her veins.

Her stomach rolled, nausea twisting her gut. Her body lurched, and her eyes bulged as understanding dawned on her. She slapped a hand over her mouth as her cheeks filled with vomit, rushing from the house into the field.

Alice doubled over at her waist, bracing her hands on her knees through her woolen skirt, and retched, freeing her stomach of its contents. When her stomach no longer flipped inside her, Alice straightened and counted on her fingers.

That could not be right.

She paused, then counted again. And again. And again, her glowing silver eyes growing even wider. Finally, her hands fell to her sides, and she stared at the water-logged field, her face a mixture of wonder and fear.

Slowly, she raised a hand to her mouth and released a sob into her palm, but it was not full of grief and pain like her earlier cries. Instead, she dropped to her knees and tilted her head back to stare at the Heavens, her silver locks floating on an unseen breeze. Tears burned the back of her eyes as her body trembled from the emotion swelling her heart. Gratitude for the gift she was only hours too late to share with her husband.

"Thank you." She hiccupped as fresh tears streamed down her cheeks. Tears of gratitude. "Mother, thank you." She crumpled on herself, overcome with emotion.

She was pregnant.

Three weeks along already. The Goddess allowed her to conceive a child, the greatest blessing she could ask for. John was gone, but part of him would remain with her. The child she would bear would be half her and half the person she loved, and Alice could not imagine something she desired more. And love filled her at the thought. And something else...

All the pain, all the grief within Alice's heart rose to the surface until she felt the emotions completely, until she faced the darkness that weighed on her. Staring her pain in the face, she acknowledged that she was just a teenage girl with the weight of the world resting on her shoulders, and that she was hurt because the only two people whom she had ever loved left her alone to carry her burdens. And then she released the pain and allowed herself to heal.

"I forgive you for leaving, John," she sobbed as she stared at the moon in the night sky above. "I forgive you, Mother, for leaving me."

Brilliant white light flashed, and an angel materialized before Alice, standing seven feet tall, with golden hair and ocean blue irises surrounding uncanny white pupils.

"Hello, Alice," he greeted her warmly, extending a large hand to her.

"G-G-Gabriel?" Alice hiccupped, accepting his massive hand that swallowed her dainty one.

Without exertion, Gabriel pulled her to standing, then released her to place his hand on her womb, where the tiniest of humans grew inside her.

"I-I-I d-do not under-understand," Alice stuttered through the congestion clogging her throat. "Why are you here?"

"I have come to unlock your earth magic, as you have passed your Water Trial."

"But I did not use any water magic—I have done nothing courageous or heroic or used my powers to save others. All I have done is cry in the dirt."

"The Trials are not always about magic, Little Bull." He rested his massive palms on either of her shoulders. "While you must master the magic, the Trial is about what you have learned from the element. It is about embodying the essence of air, fire, water, and earth, so you may one day embody the essence of Spirit."

"And I embodied the essence of water?" she asked, wiping her nose with the back of her sleeve as she sniffled.

"What do you think?" Gabriel prompted, his uncanny eyes boring into her.

Turning her head, she gazed westward to the ocean, as though she could see it through the line of trees separating her from the wharf. "I forgave them. John and my mother. Water is a soothing element, so most healers are water elementals. It cleanses and purifies us, healing our wounds. But to heal, one must confront the imbalances within themself if one is to remedy the imbalances in others."

"By forgiving them, you opened yourself to the healing of water. While you do not have the power to heal with water magic, you do have the power to choose your actions, and forgiveness is choosing to release your anger and resentment. The very act of forgiveness deals a brutal blow to the Enemy. It allows you to accept what was done and what is, and with acceptance, you can move forward. The act of forgiveness, especially when you must forgive actions that have cost you so dearly, will make you more resilient when confronted with challenges. And you will face many in your lifetime, Little Bull."

"I do not feel very resilient," she muttered, turning to the archangel.

"Perhaps not right away, but with time, it will come." He caressed her womb with both hands, like a loving father. "Rivers do not forge a new course immediately, but in time, they shift the earth to redirect their flow. And until then, you have something greater to bring you peace and joy. Congratulations, Alice. You have passed your Trial of Water. Blessed be, Little Bull."

Pressing one hand to her heart and the other to her forehead, Gabriel summoned white light to shimmer between them. The touch of Heaven burned through her, lighting her like a fire as power shattered the barrier on her magic, unleashing the element of earth. The element that had always belonged to the Nephilim flooded her body, strengthening her mind, body, and soul.

A tingling sensation swept through her hair, turning the long silver strands to their normal vibrant red. Her eyes flashed, and in an instant, they were earthly green.

Nature itself seemed to sing, welcoming her home. The world around her burst to life in vibrant colors, the energy of the flora and fauna magnified by her magic. At long last, Alice felt like she had become the witch she was always meant to be.

Running a hand over her growing belly, Alice smiled at the forest critters chirping around her. The rabbits and squirrels and chipmunks and deer and every animal of the forest had gathered around her, as they often did whenever she ventured into the forest.

Her magic, the magic of the Nephilim of Earth, called to them, and with her pregnancy progressing, Alice yearned for the company of animals more and more often. A maternal instinct rose within her when she was around her mother's beloved creatures, but perhaps it was simply that she did not feel so lonely around them, for she felt alone in her empty house without her husband to keep her company.

Her green magic danced along the treetops, rustling the branches and blooming flowers, then closing the blossoms, then opening again. Various plants grew around where she rested in the nook of a tree, and the stone of the earth quaked and shook at her command. A mere thought, and her element enacted her bidding.

She was stronger than ever, and now that she finally accessed her element, she would be unstoppable with the magic at her fingertips.

It would not be long now, she knew, until her Earth Trial began. As the daughter of the Archangel of Earth, Alice had mastered the element in a few short months, but the Trials were not her only motivation for her long, solo excursions into the woods.

While she still trained the witches on the Misery Islands, Alice found herself craving the solitude and whimsy of the woods to fully immerse herself in her element. The other witches could not possibly understand how she felt in the presence of nature, nor did she wish to explain why she spent so much time, well beyond the amount of time she spent on water magic, mingling with earth.

But dusk was setting, and while Alice did not fear the night or its creatures, for both were her lifelong companions, since her pregnancy, she treaded cautiously. She did not wish to encounter that dark entity she faced during her Fire Trial while alone and pregnant.

Her stomach rolled as she stood and said goodbye to her animal friends.

She would face the Darkness again before long.

Tossing and turning in her bed, Alice felt the straw shifting beneath her as she thrashed.

This could not be real.

But it *felt* real.

Because it was a dream vision. Alice's body was grounded firmly on the earthly plane, but her spirit ascended elsewhere, to a place where the angels could show her the past, present, or future as they deemed fit.

And in this moment, Alice knew she saw the future, something that had not yet happened but would, if she continued down her current path.

This was a warning granted to Alice by her mother, Uriel.

A warning she would not ignore like she did the last.

Alice saw herself, at three years old, running through the forest to a meadow enclosed by a circle of trees. The sun beamed on her, its light filtering through the canopy of branches and leaves. A warm, gentle breeze blew past her, lovingly caressing her skin as forest animals ran alongside her.

A woman, near identical in looks to Alice but a few years older than Alice was now, followed young Alice through the forest path.

No, the little girl was not Alice.

She was Alice's *daughter*. The child she carried in her womb, she realized with a start.

Dream-Alice had survived the Salem War. The magnitude of her powers could be seen in how nature reached for her, eager to touch the Salem Witch as she watched her daughter play, a smile dancing on her lips.

With a frown, dream-Alice looked up at the sky.

Storm clouds gathered overhead as thunder rolled through the sky. She had not called the storm, and it came on too suddenly to be natural.

Indigo lightning crashed through the trees, striking the ground in front of dream-Alice. The force of the impact blew Alice off her feet, throwing her away from her daughter.

Alice watched in terror as the earth rose around her future self, the soil rising over her head, pulling dream-Alice deeper and deeper into a tomb of earth. Another bolt of indigo lightning cracked through the sky, striking the young girl just feet away.

Lunging forward, Alice made to shield the child with her body, but the lightning merely passed through her, blasting into the girl. At her feet laid the child, her hunter green eyes open and vacant.

An agonized scream tore from her throat at the sight of her daughter dead before her.

Another bolt of lightning struck the ground, and John's corpse appeared beside their daughter, lying in a puddle of salt water. Water leaked from his insides, his water-logged body swollen and soggy, his lips blue and his face pale.

Falling to her hands and knees, Alice dug her fingers into the soil, churning the earth under her hands.

This could not be. John could not be... her dream vision. The one where the Darkness claimed John's life... it had finally come to pass, as would the death of her daughter if she did not heed this warning.

Indigo light flashed, and that Darkness, the same one that stole her husband in her dream vision, appeared before Alice. Seething, she clamored to her feet, raising her hands to summon the elements, but they did not answer her, for the elements did not exist in the realm of dreams. Tendrils of darkness rose from the ground, wrapping around her defenseless body like snakes.

The Darkness lurched for her, and her vision went black.

Rocketing upright in bed, Alice gasped for breath, pressing one hand to her chest and the other to her swollen belly. Panting, she closed her eyes, trying to slow her beating heart before it hammered out of her chest.

Slipping from between the sheets, Alice wrapped a wool shawl around her shoulders, then gently padded out the door, her feet bare against the earth.

She had always loved the sensation of the soil between her toes, but since she unlocked her earth magic—the magic of her mother— she felt more connected to Heaven. The touch of the element against her bare skin soothed her in a way she could not describe.

As she walked into the forest, the trees swayed, their branches reaching toward their beloved witch. Everywhere her feet touched, green and gold magic swirled, blossoming forth fresh plants.

Even as her mind roamed and her eyes glazed over, Alice's feet knew the way. She had long since walked this route to the ocean. Her toes wiggled in the sand as she reached the beach. At night, she and John would sneak out of their houses, and meet here, then silently row to the Misery Islands to practice in secret.

But now, she was alone, gazing up at the full moon shining on her, its light glinting off the calm ocean surface.

A hand trailed lightly over her baby bulge. Six months pregnant. She was not alone. This child—a daughter, she had seen a daughter in the vision—belonged to her. Solace in her time of grief. Yet soon after her birth, she, too, would be stolen from Alice.

All the powers of darkness could not stop Alice, and she would not allow evil to win again. The world stole her husband. It would not take her daughter, too.

Her daughter could not remain in Salem.

If it saved her child's life, gave her a chance to live—to freely practice magic, perhaps—Alice would send her away.

But with whom? Whom did Alice have faith in to entrust her daughter to them? Who would willingly leave their family and friends and home to risk their lives while spiriting Alice's daughter away in secrecy?

Elizabeth Bradbury. The name floated through her mind, the words spoken by Uriel.

Elizabeth Bradbury's husband passed recently, so she planned to leave Salem with her children in search of a fresh start and probably another husband. There were no available men of witch descent, and it was suicide to attempt to engage in a relationship with a human.

It made sense for Elizabeth to take Ariel with her.

Alice ran a hand over her swollen belly, caressing the skin cocooning the child growing within her womb.

Elizabeth was a warm and loving mother, and Alice had faith she would care for her unborn daughter. But that did not make the decision any easier.

With the help of her parents and perhaps Thomas Bradbury, Elizabeth's father, Alice would convince the townsfolk to believe her child died in the birthing bed. As the leader of the witches of Salem, her word surpassing the Athenian Council's, Alice held the loyalty of the people, but given the severity of her vision... no, she could not trust the other witches with this secret.

The ruse was not a far stretch. Women and children often died in the birthing bed, though humans typically more so than witches, since magical healers could save a mortal from the brink of death.

Closing her eyes in sullen defeat, a single tear leaked from the Nephilim's eye. Alice would not raise her daughter, just as Uriel had not been permitted to raise Alice.

CHAPTER SIX

THE STRENGTH OF EARTH

Alice lay in a straw bed, her forehead beaded with sweat and tears flowing down her cheeks. The expression on her face was not one of pain—it was one of agony. Both her hair and eyes glimmered silver rather than her natural look of fiery red hair and hunter green eyes.

Alice cursed Gabriel for his timing. What twisted mind thought to overlap her Earth Trial with childbirth? She was going to kill that angel when she saw him.

She gripped Martha's hand tightly as she contracted, releasing a vicious groan.

Life cannot exist without pain. You were a fierce labor, my child, as all the powerful are. This child was touched by an angel while growing in your womb, so she is more powerful than a normal half Nephilim. And more power always causes more pain, Uriel spoke into Alice's mind so only she could hear. Even from a realm away, Uriel never abandoned Alice. *This immense pain is the price we pay to harness the power to bring a new life into the world. Women have a unique ability. In a sense, the power of the Goddess flows through us, so the Spirit of the Creator uses us as vessels to merge a soul into its human body.*

Alice screamed in agony, her magic shaking the house as she pushed harder. She gripped the hand of her adoptive mother, Martha, so tightly that both their knuckles turned white, but Martha hardly noticed as she spoke encouragement to her adoptive daughter. Alice pushed and pushed until a tiny, beautiful baby's head emerged, filling the room with its high-pitched cries.

"One more time, dear," Martha encouraged Alice excitedly. "One more push."

Alice obliged, releasing a blood-curdling scream as the rest of the baby's body slid free. Crumpling into the pillows, Alice gulped down heavy breaths. The midwife administering the birth gripped the crying baby firmly, yet gently, and wrapped a clean cotton around the little one.

"It is a girl, Miss Alice," the midwife announced.

Covered in a sheen of sweat, Alice smiled as the midwife gently transitioned the crying newborn into Alice's arms. Pulling her to her breast, Alice cradled the babe in her arms, and the pain in her groin vanished.

Martha moved to the end of the bed while the midwife fussed over Alice and the babe. Blue light flashed between Alice's legs as Martha used her healing magic—she was a water witch and a healer who relearned her powers in the last years as Alice mastered her own.

The painful ache diminished entirely as Martha's magic soothed and healed. Childbirth was a war of its own, and not one easily waged in this century. But with magic, witches were blessed with superior recovery. If only they were not so afraid of witches, humans could benefit from the magic of healers.

But from the moment Alice held her daughter in her arms, the pain did not register in her mind. What pain could compare to the joy of holding one's child for the first time?

Alice's eyes sparkled like gemstones, the green brighter than ever. Maternal instinct swelled in Alice as an overwhelming sense of love and affection flooded her chest, and for the first time since losing John, Alice felt whole. But the desire to hold her daughter forever, to never let her go, gripped Alice's heart, yet she would do whatever it took to protect the precious human in her arms.

In our weakest moments, we find our strength. Find the strength to save your daughter, Alice. The voice of Alice's birth mother drifted through her mind, reminding her of the dark warnings she received in her dream visions. Visions that she would not ignore again.

"Mother." Tearing her eyes away from her little girl, Alice beckoned Martha to join her at the head of the bed. "Have you gathered the others?"

Martha hesitated before nodding stiffly.

"Good." She signed in relief. "They must leave at once."

Martha's expression soured. "Alice, darling, do you really think this is necessary? Your daughter does not yet have a name. She was just born for Lord's sake. How do you expect her to survive the journey?"

Alice stared fondly at her little girl. "You are right," she whispered. "She needs a name."

Martha rolled her eyes and muttered under her breath, "Not the most important point I made. Dear Lord, help us."

"How about Ariel?" Alice spoke softly to her daughter, who upon hearing her name, quieted her crying, as if the name itself brought her peace.

"Ariel Martha Parker," Alice announced to Martha and the midwife, who scribbled the name on a birth document, then slipped out the door to return with Giles in tow.

At her adoptive mother's shocked expression, Alice explained, "For both my mothers."

Tears welled in Martha's eyes as she wrapped both mother and daughter in a tender embrace. Overcome with emotion, neither spoke, only held each other and the newborn babe. Maiden. Mother. Crone. Each female represented a different aspect of the Goddess, and the symbolism was a power within itself.

Lumbering over to his daughter, Giles stared at the bundled baby girl in her arms, a tear welling in his eye. Alice's adoptive father had never been one for emotion, but even he was touched by the sentimentality.

Martha pulled away, wiping the tears rolling down her cheeks with the sleeve of her wool dress. She sniffled. "Is this necessary? Must we be separated from her?"

Alice's face filled with grief as she stared at her little girl cradled in her arms. "If there was any other way, I would not hesitate. But I have seen it, as I saw it with John. If I ignore this dream—this vision—then I will be no better a mother than I was a wife. This is the only way to save her.... Besides, it is not forever."

Alice lowered her lips to Ariel's forehead and lightly brushed them over her soft, damp skin in a kiss. She whispered softly, so only her newborn daughter heard, "Know you are loved, my beautiful daughter, by more people than you know. And one day, I will come for you. I love you more than the Earth itself, and I will travel to Eden and back to find you."

A solid knock rapped on the door.

"Who is it?" Giles barked.

"Thomas Bradbury."

Wrenching the door open, Giles ushered the man inside and shook his hand. Thomas nodded to Martha, a grim expression on his face, as he strode to Alice's bedside, offering her a fatherly smile. "Hello there, Miss Alice. And who might this little fella be?"

Alice laughed lightly, not taking her eyes off her beautiful daughter. A beautiful daughter with hunter green eyes. The granddaughter of Archangel Uriel. "This is Ariel, my newborn baby girl."

"Ah," Thomas sighed. "John would have been mighty happy to have a girl. Looks like her mother."

"You think?" Alice gazed lovingly at Ariel as her eyes drooped, the newborn lulling to sleep in her mother's arms.

"Yes, Ma'am. And thank the Lord for that. Would not want her to take after John, would we?" he teased with a smile.

Giles snorted from behind Thomas, covering his laugh with a cough.

Waiting, Thomas allowed Alice a few minutes with her daughter before clearing his throat. "Miss Alice... Elizabeth is waiting out front with the others. It... well, it is time."

A sob bubbled in Alice's chest, and she choked, fighting the fresh tears streaming down her face. "I know," she sobbed. "I know it is temporary, but..."

Another knock sounded against the wooden door, softer than Thomas's.

Martha called, "Who is it?"

"It is me," a woman's voice called. "Elizabeth Bradbury."

Martha hurriedly let in a woman around forty years of age. Exchanging short pleasantries, Elizabeth hurried to join her father at Alice's bedside, and Alice choked on another sob, knowing what Elizabeth's presence meant. All of Salem believed Elizabeth had already departed, but it was a ruse.

"Goody," she spoke the nickname gently, her features softening. "I am sorry, but there is no time to waste. We must leave now if we are to succeed."

"I know," Alice sobbed, her voice almost a wail.

Thomas clapped Elizabeth on the shoulder as he said, "Now, Miss Alice, my daughter here will take fine care of your Ariel. This is not her first time caring for a child, and you cannot ask for a better woman to look after your little one."

As fresh tears rolled down her cheeks, Alice hummed a melodious tune, one her celestial mother sang to her in her infancy. Alice did not know how she knew it, only that a certain ethereal feeling settled over her, like her mother was present in the room.

Born of Light, all the angels are assembled,
With hair like fire and eyes of emeralds,
In you, all of Heaven and Earth shall delight.
Safe with others, in your flight,

You will be saved from Darkness's plight.
And blessed forever with the Goddess's Light.
Descent of Uriel, you are blessed by Earth,
May your days and nights be filled with mirth.
Nature shall always protect Its child,
Until the day you and I are reconciled.

As Alice ended her blessing, Elizabeth stretched her arms out. "Goody, please..." she prompted. "Can you give her to me?"

Reluctantly, the new mother handed Ariel to Elizabeth with painstaking slowness. An eternity passed as she wrestled with the pain of separating from her child. When Ariel was out of her hands and in Elizabeth's arms, Alice collapsed in a heap. Giles tried to console her with a fatherly hug, but she cried harder as she gripped him back, her fingertips digging into his arm.

"Her name..." she said through the tremorous sobs wracking her body. "Her name is Ariel Martha."

Elizabeth's clear blue eyes met Alice's hunter green gaze as she said, "It is a strong name for a strong girl. Like her mother, and her mothers. I will love her with all my heart, as Martha has loved you."

Alice managed a nod as she cried into Giles's shoulder, her tears staining his outer coat. Without another word, Elizabeth turned and walked out the door held open by Martha. The midwife hurried after her, carrying a canvas bag of necessities for the child.

With a tip of his hat, Thomas followed the two women out of the house, no doubt to see his daughter and grandchildren off before they embarked on their treacherous journey.

When they were gone, Martha climbed into the blood-soaked bed and wrapped her arms around her daughter, allowing Alice to fall into her chest to be consoled.

"Shh," she whispered, stroking Alice's hair. "Shh, my dear. We must wait until they are good and gone before you can be heard. Then you may be as loud as you want. Wake the entire village if you must. But you must be strong."

Alice could only nod, the grief of her loss screaming from every fiber in her being. If all her self-control was not focused on containing herself, containing her emotions so her magic did not detonate and summon an army of demons like the one that attacked during her Fire Trial, Alice could have wrapped the house in an impenetrable bubble of silence with her air magic. But if she let herself go, even for a moment, she would lose the war with her heartbreak, and that monster, the demonic dark entity she faced that night, would sense her distraught and seek her out to feed on her depression.

It was as though she were struck by lightning as her magic zapped through her. Gasping, Alice rocketed upright in bed, tearing out of her mother's arms.

"It is here," she declared, her sickly pale face lightening another shade.

She kept her magic contained, so how did it find her?

"What is here?" Alarmed, Martha rose from the bed, scanning the house for an indication of a threat. "Alice, what is wrong?"

Alice leapt from the bed, then swayed. Giles extended a hand to assist, but as Alice's bare feet brushed against the earthen floor, her mother's element rushed into her, steadying her. "Do you remember my Fire Trial? The dark entity that attacked us. It is here."

"How do you know?" Giles demanded, summoning air magic to his hands.

"My range to detect magical signature extends much farther than yours. And its presence is not one that I could mistake," she replied, placing a calming hand on Giles's forearm, urging him to lower his magic-filled hands. Alice would not allow her parents to face this Darkness.

It was after her. Intuition slammed into Alice's gut.

No. It was after Ariel.

She stomped to the door, summoning the four elements to swirl around her, ready to do her bidding.

"Alice, wait." Martha rushed after her to place a gentle hand on her shoulder. "You cannot face this Darkness alone."

"I must," Alice said, her voice resolute. "It seeks my daughter. Even now, I can feel its dark tendrils searching for her magic. If it discovers she has fled, it will chase her and consume her and the others."

"What does it want with Ariel?" Giles grumbled in his deep baritone.

"It senses her power." Alice met her father's eye. "With one Nephilim parent, the blood of angels runs through her veins, and it makes her powerful. Possibly more powerful than any witch in Salem other than me. I do not know its goal, but this entity will not suffer a being stronger than it to live in this world."

"What are you going to do?" Martha asked fearfully.

"I will face it," Alice said with unwavering authority. "If I cannot defeat it, then I will distract it until Ariel is far enough away that he cannot sense her powers and track her."

"Alice," Giles spoke her name in warning, always the overprotective father. "You just gave birth. And while Martha healed you, you are not at full strength."

Palming a lock of her hair, Alice held up the shining silver strands. "I beg to argue, Father. The touch of the angel has blessed me with an exorbitant amount of power. I am as powerful as I was at the beginning of this Trial." She spun on her heel, marching for the door. Resting her hand on the handle, she paused. "Do not try to stop me, and do not try to help me, for the Darkness will consume you. I will protect you with holy flames, but for your safety, do not leave this house until I return. That is a command from your Reigning Salem Witch." Alice stared them each in the eye until they nodded, conceding to her commands.

This was her war, and she was the general.

Wrenching the door open, she stepped into the night, wearing her blood-stained dress, her feet bare against the earth. Her magic extended from her in a shockwave, sensing the forest creatures fleeing as the dark entity approached from the forest to the north.

In eerie silence, not a forest creature to be seen or heard, Alice waited patiently for the Darkness as it crept closer. A misty fog rolled into the clearing from the forest surrounding the house. It was not natural, but Alice was not afraid.

Raising a flat hand in the air, she sent a mild squall to brush away the fog, giving her a clear line of sight at the trees where she knew it lingered.

From the shadows emerged the same dark entity she faced during her Fire Trial. An undulating mass of indigo darkness. And once again, Alice would fight this evil being.

But she was worried despite what she told her parents. She just gave birth. Blood still soaked her dress, and though her eyes and hair were silver, the physical toll of childbirth was a traumatic ordeal.

Yet, Alice did not flinch as the dark entity released a guttural roar and surged toward her in a blur.

White fire burst from her hands, launching at the enemy. But it dodged at the last second, pivoting around Alice's attack, still on a path to attack her.

Summoning water from the damp air, Alice snapped a whip of water at the dark entity. Cracking against its outer shell, the shock of pain forced the enemy back.

But Alice remembered their last fight.

Her attacks had been futile until she snuck *inside* the Darkness and unleashed an inferno.

Power raged inside her like a typhoon, waiting to be freed from her body which caged it. Alice released her power in the form of the elements.

Air lashed out of her. Then fire. Then water. Then earth. The elements plowed into the Darkness, one after the other, each blow forcing the enemy to retreat a step.

Spooking, Alice reappeared behind the Darkness and bombarded her enemy with the four elements from behind, earning an agonized roar from the Darkness.

Inky tendrils of indigo magic shot toward her, piercing through her elemental attacks to sail toward her physical body. Spooking into the forest, she narrowly avoided being skewered by the Darkness.

She spooked again to approach the entity from another angle. And again and again, Alice spooked, attacked, then dodged the Darkness's evil tentacles by spooking. And on and on they danced, exchanging blows.

But Alice had the upper hand, unrelenting in her elemental storm that bombarded the enemy, until at last, she decided to deal the final, devastating blow.

Spooking one last time, she disappeared from where she stood on the ground to re-materialize in the air above the dark entity. She dropped.

Alice braced herself, willing the earth below to soften the impact when she landed on the ground inside the Darkness, same as in her Fire Trial.

But Alice had overcalculated her hand.

The enemy raised an inky dark tentacle, expanding and morphing until it formed a paddle.

It swiped, smashing into Alice's side and throwing her violently through the air. She smacked against the roof of her house, the force of impact shattering the shingles as she skidded over the wood.

Groaning, Alice rolled to all fours and touched a hand to her spinning head. She felt like she would retch.

Sensing with magic rather than seeing with her eyes, Alice detected the dark entity rise in the air and rush toward her.

She dropped, pressing her body flat against the roof as she summoned holy flames to shield her back, searing the enemy as it descended on her. It reared back, and Alice summoned a squall to throw it off her and to the ground below.

"You do not scare me," Alice growled, rising to her feet as the magic of the elements danced around her. "I met evil when I was merely a child. And a child I am no longer."

She was a woman. A warrior. And now a mother.

Stepping off the edge of the roof, she dropped to the ground once more to fight. Air slapped the stewing darkness. Fire burned, water flowed, earth quaked. Element after element pummeled the enemy, forcing it back with every step Alice took forward. Wind raged around her in a cyclone, white flames burned untamed, water poured in sheets from the sky, and earth rumbled under her feet as vines burst forth from the soil to attack the enemy. All the while, Alice pursued the Darkness.

If she could get inside it, she could unleash the power of the four elements simultaneously and vaporize the Darkness. She could...

A beam of indigo light shot from the enemy and slammed into her chest, throwing her. Agony lanced through her entire body as the dark energy sought to devour her.

Tumbling heels over head, Alice smacked into the side of the house, her head crashing painfully against the corner of a beam. Tumbling to the ground, she barely summoned a wind to dull her fall, but the impact forced the air from her lungs.

Demonic magic rushed over her skin, trying to burrow into her soul. It was going to overcome her, and she would be lost to this beast for all eternity. She was not strong enough in her weakened state. Weakened by the physical toll of childbirth and the agonizing loss of her daughter.

As the blackness crept in, Alice could not find within herself the will to live. What did life have to offer her? More pain and loss? A life without her husband and child? Alice had nothing left and nothing left to gain. She would yield to the might of her enemy this night.

Earth is finding your strength when you have nothing left. It is hitting rock bottom and using it as the solid foundation on which you rise again. Uriel's voice drifted through Alice's head. After all, this was the Trial of her mother's element. *You are stronger now than the last time you faced this evil. Unleash your demons in the form of the elements and repel this beast to protect your daughter while she flees. She is your reason. Salem is your reason. The world is your reason to survive, to fight.*

The power of Uriel's voice and the wisdom of her words sank into Alice, singing to her soul, and despite the pain, despite her hopelessness, Alice remembered who she was and to whom she belonged. She was the Nephilim daughter of Earth and the Salem Witch. She was a Daughter of Heaven, chosen by the Goddess herself, tasked by the Creator to protect its creation. She was a witch and a woman and a wife and a mother, and she would not be shaken.

Breathless, Alice summoned the fire of Heaven to swallow her in a bonfire of holy flames that incinerated the indigo magic threatening to ravage her mind, body, and soul, earning a glass-shattering shriek from her enemy.

Sucking in a blessed breath, Alice struggled to her hands and knees. Gingerly, she touched a hand to the back of her head, where blood flowed from a gash in her scalp.

That blast of magic... it was not merely demonic... it was too powerful. It was borderline satanic.

Alice's head snapped up. Could it be...?

Only nine creatures of Hell could wield such magic, and Alice knew this was neither Lucifer nor Lilith, so it must have been one of the Seven.

If it was, Alice had more to fear for her daughter than she initially thought. She could not simply stall this soldier of evil. She must beat it so thoroughly it could not rise. Alice must fight like she had never fought before. But never before had she felt such unwavering motivation to fight.

For Ariel.

Shoving to her feet, Alice faced her enemy with a resiliency only embodied by earth. "I know what you are," she growled, her hands curling into fists at her side.

And she knew how to beat back this darkness.

Until she unlocked her powers of Spirit, she could not permanently end her enemy, but with the blood of angels running through her veins and the kiss of Heaven upon her brow as the Salem Witch, she could win tonight's battle.

Calling upon the purity of her soul, the piece of Spirit magic she always had access to, for one could never be truly separated from one's soul, she summoned the elements to swirling in a ball between her raised hands.

The dark entity charged in a frenzy to stop her from executing her angelic magic.

Reaching into her gut, Alice tugged on the power inherent to her. The power granted to her by the blood of angels and the mark of the Goddess that blessed her silver features.

The enemy was feet away, its form blurred from the speed of its attack.

Penetrating green light poured from Alice's palms, joining with the elements. With a violent thrust, Alice shoved her hands forward, smacking them into the enemy as it reached her, that satanic indigo light reaching for her to devour her soul.

Green light glowed between them, blasting through the dark tendrils that stretched for Alice and clawing into the enemy's body.

It screeched in pain, pulling away, but the elements held steadfast, rooting the enemy to where it hovered above the ground as air, fire, water, and earth followed the green light to assault the Darkness from within.

Alice's silver eyes flashed in the moonlight.

Every ounce of rage and loss and grief inside of her funneled from her chest, down her arms, and into the magic rocketing from her palms. Emotion fueled her magic, and her magic was as strong as she was.

But she had more.

Alice poured more of herself into the magic, holding the enemy with an iron grip as it struggled to squirm out of her grasp. The power of the elements, combined with her angelic magic, was torture to the enemy, and the more she caused it pain, the more intent Alice became. Intent on destroying this beast that sought to ruin her and the ones she loved.

The energy in her gut—her sea of chi—pumped through her veins with more fervor than before. But for every shock of pain she inflicted on her enemy, more and more power vanished from her energy stores.

With resolve in her heart and steely mettle in her eyes, Alice summoned the last of her magic all at once, calling it to the surface, swelling like a tsunami until only a drop remained in her core.

Releasing an unearthly battle cry, her voice layered with the voices of the archangels whose magic filled her, and Alice unleashed the last of her magic.

The elements detonated like a bomb.

The force of her own attack slammed into Alice, throwing her backward. Sailing through the air, Alice allowed herself to smash into the side of the house, then fall to the ground, too tired to summon a wisp of air to cushion the impacts.

By will power alone, Alice pushed to her forearms, staring at the place the Darkness just been. But it was not there. Alice's silver eyes cut to the tree line where her enemy slunk into the shadows, moving slowly, like a wounded animal.

For Alice dealt a devastating blow to the beast. It would not rise again tonight to follow Ariel. Nausea rolled in her gut, and Alice knew her daughter was safe, for the enemy would not recover from Alice's fierce attack any time soon.

But it *would* recover, and it would come for her.

With shaking arms, Alice struggled to her feet. Her appendages felt like lead, but the physical exhaustion was nothing compared to her emotional fatigue.

More than the battle weighed on her.

Shoulders hunched, Alice trudged into the house, entirely spent of her magic, and collapsed into the bed, gripping her mother tightly as she sobbed into Martha's wool dress.

She lost her daughter and almost lost this fight and her life. She almost gave up. And Alice knew she could not lose the next battle, or the world would fall into darkness. It was so much pressure on the shoulders of a sixteen-year-old woman. After she had endured so much. Part of her wanted the Trials to end her, but the other part... the other part remembered from whom her strength came. The Creator was within her. She would not fail.

"Hello, Alice," Gabriel's deep timbre cut through the wooden shack, startling her parents, but Alice merely stared at him with lightless eyes.

"By the Creator," Martha said, scrambling from the bed to kneel beside her husband, their fists clapped over their hearts in a show of reverence for the Messenger Archangel.

Alice did not stir as her glare cut into Gabriel like glass. She had lost everything. First her husband, now her daughter, and if her visions were correct, she would lose more before this war was finished.

Gabriel's uncanny white-pupiled vision slid from Alice to her companions. "Rise, Martha. Rise, Giles." When the mortals rose, he strode to them and placed a massive hand on each of their shoulders. "Dark times lie ahead. You do not yet know the evil you face. You can run now, flee with Ariel and save yourselves, or you can stay and fight. But if you do, you must prepare yourselves to lose what you cherish most."

Martha did not waver. "I have faith in Alice. She will claim victory in the name of Heaven."

"She will," Gabriel agreed, an ominous tone lacing his words. "But not without sacrifice. I cannot tell you the future, but know it is shrouded in darkness. Can you endure it?"

Both mortals nodded, uncertainty flashing through their eyes, but was quickly replaced with determination.

"I will stay by my daughter's side until my final breath," Martha declared.

Giles crossed his massive arms over his chest. "I have lived a long life, most of it in this town. I will not be run out by dark cretins. If Alice must face this darkness, then so shall I."

Gabriel nodded, but Alice did not miss the sorrow in his ocean blue eyes as he patted the mortals on their shoulders.

"Alice, you have remained strong, making the choices necessary instead of the ones you desired. You chose the good of others before yourself and did not waver in your decision, even as you lost your daughter and the last piece of your husband in order to save her life." Fresh tears flowed down Alice's cheeks at the archangel's words. "Uriel is proud. Few understand the spirit of earth, but as her daughter, you embody the strength of the element beyond any mortal. This was only the beginning. You will face abominable darkness and consequential decisions in your Salem War, and even after, should you choose. Congratulations Alice, you have passed your Trial of Earth."

Leaning over the bed, Gabriel placed his right hand on Alice's heart and his left to the crown of her forehead. Heaven's white light poured from his palms, seeping into Alice as the magic of the Goddess swept through her body, crashing through the last barrier to her magic.

Spirit magic. The magic she had always known, because it was in her very soul. Unbelievable power, which could only come from the Creator, rushed through Alice's body, filling every dark corner of her soul. Divine power obliterated the stone wall that withheld the full power of the Salem Witch, and Spirit pulsed within her, tingling her skin as it ached to extend beyond her body.

Alice's fingers twitched with the need to use her magic, even as Spirit healed the last of the pain lashing through her. Golden wisps of Spirit wafted off her body as though she was a flame in the dark. Heat engulfed her, but it was not unpleasant as the element baptized her in its power. Raw power that was capable of demolishing the Darkness threatening this world.

Golden lightning—the manifestation of Spirit magic—crackled to life around her in a brilliant display of power. Calling her power to her body, Alice absorbed the lightning and locked it tightly in her core of swirling magic.

Her eyelids fluttered open in a flash of hunter green, but what were once twinkling green orbs were now lifeless, dull blobs. Alice collapsed into the bed as the last strands of hair reverted to their normal fiery red, signaling the completion of her Trial.

But she did not collapse from lack of power.

No, she possessed plenty of power. It was the grief of loss that incapacitated Alice, so she could not bear to rise.

But she must.

Because tonight she did not face an ordinary demon. No lesser demon, not even a greater demon, could wield such potent dark magic. Only a Prince of Hell, one of the seven angels who fell from Heaven at Lucifer's command, could withstand the powers of the Salem Witch.

And Alice finally knew whom she would wage her Salem War against.

One of the Seven Deadly Sins.

IMPRISONED

Snow blanketed Salem, the freshly fallen powder making the town glisten under the cold winter sun. Flakes drifted lazily from the sky, in no more of a hurry than the townsfolk milling about, enjoying the shining sun despite the frigid temperatures. Many people hustled from one place to another, eager to limit their exposure to the cold and find comfort in the warmth indoors. It was the first day of March, and the weather had yet to thaw, but the shining sun was a blessing after so many gray days.

A woman's scream pierced the air.

Alice spun away from the door to the butcher's shop, her sharp green eyes landing on two men dragging a dark-skinned woman through the slush.

Each man held her arm with an iron grip. One man stood above six feet, with a wide chest and an even wider stomach. White-gray hair peaked out from under a wool cap, and he dressed in fine clothes as one of the wealthy in town. His eyes were brown, dark enough to be mistaken for black, and glinting with malicious intent, like he enjoyed pulling the thrashing woman down the street.

Alice recognized him immediately as her magic surged to life, almost jumping off her skin with the desire to attack him before he could hurt her. Her magic screamed that something about him was not human. No, he was not inhuman—he was *less* than human.

As he looked down at the woman as he dragged her through the street, his lips twisted into a vindictive smirk, and Alice sensed he lusted for more. He craved the pain the woman felt, as though inflicting torture gave him power.

The other man, by comparison, could not have been more opposite. Where the first man was large and foreboding, the second man embodied the appearance of a weasel. His stature was short and scrawny, nothing more than a skeleton covered in a layer of loose skin with a head disproportionately smaller than his body. The bags under his sunken cheeks made his black beady eyes seem void of any life.

"Magistrate John Hathorne and Reverend Jonathon Corwin, two of the vilest men to walk this earth," the butcher grumbled under his breath.

Martha and Giles stiffened beside Alice. Alice knew they did not disagree with the butcher, but they did not want to be associated with those who denied the rich and powerful of the town for fear of their hammer raining down on the Coreys.

But Alice held no such tentativeness. If she could get her hands on the little rodents, she could... she could not do anything.

Alice was so used to being the one everybody looked to in a crisis since the night she saved the witches from the demon attack during her Fire Trial, but in public, Alice was as useless as a witch without magic.

Men and women flooded the streets as the dark-skinned woman screamed again. Despite the cold, every person in the town rushed to discover the source of the noise. The crowd gathering around Hathorne and Corwin grew so thick, the family could no longer see the two men and their hostage.

Ignoring her parents as they cried after her, Alice leapt off the stone step to the shop and charged into the crowd, who parted from the power of her presence. Martha trotted after Alice, her features pinched in concern as Giles and the butcher followed suit. As Alice waded through the mass of bodies, her air magic sang to her, carrying the voices of the people she sought at the center of the crowd.

"That is her Reverend," a voice—belonging to a young girl from the sounds of it—shouted from somewhere in the crowd. "She is the witch."

Alice nearly stopped in her tracks from the shock.

The crowd gasped in horror. Several humans scrambled backward, as if putting distance between themselves and the accused witch would somehow prevent them from becoming afflicted with the Devil's touch. But why were they surprised? Had not the witches foreseen this years ago? Unflinchingly, Alice strode forward.

"It is true, Magistrate," another little girl squeaked. "I witnessed the entire thing. Tituba is a witch, evil incarnate, serving Satan."

"What is going on here?" Alice's fierce voice barked as she stormed through the front line of people crowded around the two men and their prisoner, her red hair billowing from under her winter bonnet, making her head appear on fire.

Tituba laid shivering in the snow at Alice's feet. Whether from the cold or fear, Alice did not know.

"Magistrate. Reverend." Alice acknowledged the men with two stiff nods. "I beg of you, pray tell what reason you have to abduct this woman from her home and drag her through the street like a criminal?"

Corwin scoffed, "Young lady, you have no right to question—"

Hathorne waved him off. "Now, now, Reverend. The woman asks a valid question, one I fully intend to supply an answer to. You see, my fellow citizens, this creature"—he stabbed a finger at where Tituba lay crumpled at his feet—"this creature is a servant of the Devil... a WITCH," he shouted for the gathered crowd to hear.

"No, sir, please," Tituba begged from where she lay in the snow. "I ain't do nothin' of the sort." Tears streamed down her cheeks as she clasped her hands together in prayer.

Corwin spat at her. "Silence, witch."

Alice hid her hands in her skirts as they curled into fists. Her body shook from rage, but she hoped anyone who noticed attributed it to the cold.

The woman was innocent, but as a slave, it was too easy for the townsfolk to take the word of two children over Tituba's. As a woman, Alice's word was almost as useless as Tituba's, but she was the Salem Witch, and she would not turn her back on this woman—a woman who Alice knew for certain was not a witch as she possessed no magical powers.

Not that she could tell the townsfolk.

Alice's face was a mask of steel, her fierce green eyes and wild red hair turning her into a fearsome sight. "And what proof do you claim to leverage against this woman? Other than the word of two little girls." Alice gestured to the girls, not bothering to glance in their direction, showing how little weight their opinions held.

When Hathorne and Corwin failed to answer, Alice scowled. "As I thought." She started for Tituba, but Hathorne stepped in her path, standing toe-to-toe with the Salem Witch.

If only she could use her powers...

"Now Ma'am, we do not know what evidence there may be against this woman, but that is why there will be a trial—to display the evidence against her and determine whether she is a servant of the Lord or a servant of Satan."

Corwin scoffed. "Not likely to be a servant of the Lord. Never have I seen this one attend a single mass."

"Considering she is a slave of Reverend Paris, I doubt you would," Alice snapped.

"Like I said," Hathorne frowned at the unexpected defense of Tituba. "There will be a trial to determine her guilt—"

"Or innocence," Alice countered with ice on her tone.

"Or innocence," Hathorne ground the words out through bared teeth. "Until then, she will remain in a prison cell."

"No." Alice stepped forward, as if she could physically stop the men from taking her. And she could. She was the Salem Witch, the

Nephilim daughter of Uriel. Alice could put the heavy-set man on his backside, but...

Giles's meaty hand wrapped around his daughter's elbow, pulling her back the step. Glancing around the circle of gathered townspeople, dismay filled her chest as she realized if she struck him down, she would cause more problems for Tituba and for herself.

Reluctantly, Alice retreated into the safety of her parents' arms, conceding to the despicable men. The men hauled Tituba up by her arms once more, but instead of struggling, Tituba hung limply between them, her knees dragging through the snow and mud as the fight left her and she resigned herself to her fate.

The Coreys, the butcher, and other townsfolk stared bitterly after them. Slowly the crowd dispersed, but Alice's magic sensed most of the stragglers were witches. With a shake of her head and subtle wave of her hand, the witches left to not bring attention to themselves.

Alice turned on her heel, snow crunching under her foot as she took Martha's arm and trotted along the snow-covered path out of town and toward the family's estate, Giles stomping after them. When they were a distance away from any townsfolk, Alice and Martha broke into a whispered conversation, sheltered by Alice's air magic so none could eavesdrop, even with magic.

"This is a problem." Alice scowled savagely. "More so than I had anticipated."

"Thank the Lord the woman they accused isn't actually a witch."

"That fact only makes this all the more concerning."

Martha pursed her lips. "What do you mean?"

"They are not interested in rounding up those of us who possess magic. As it stands, we do not know what their goal is. And the fact that Putnam's daughter was with the accusers today... their involvement does not sit well with me."

"Therefore, we are ignorant of what game we are playing and its rules," Martha concluded. "What are we going to do about Tituba?"

Alice frowned pensively, glaring at the snow as they trekked home. "We do whatever we can to clear her name. If we do not, they will surely condemn her."

"Not that I want to see the woman dead. She does not deserve such a fate, but if you openly defy her trial, they will come after you."

"I am well aware. However, if Tituba is condemned, Hathorne and Corwin will sentence her to death, but it will not be long before they offer her a trade—her life exchanged for the names of other witches. And like in the Old World, these witch hunts will escalate and spiral beyond reach of control. If we do not stop this now, then we are all doomed."

"But Tituba is not a witch."

"It does not matter. This is a ploy for power—only I am not sure to what end. We must tread cautiously, for it will not be long before those *children* accuse more townsfolk of dabbling in witchcraft."

Martha paused, studying her daughter. Placing a hand on Alice's cheek, she stared into her earthy green eyes. "Forgive me, daughter. I see now that your decision to send Ariel away was wise. Wise beyond your years." She frowned as she tucked a stray red lock behind Alice's ear. "I wish I could have spared you this responsibility."

Alice sighed, placing her hand over her mother's. "Sometimes I wish that, too, but someone must, and I am grateful no other must carry this burden."

Glancing over her shoulder at the town, Alice's eye caught a dark blob moving toward them at a clipped pace. Her eyes narrowed in suspicion. Following her stared, Giles stepped in front of the two women, shielding them with his larger body. Uncertainty rolled off Alice's parents. Tituba's arrest rattled them, but Alice would not let it shake her. She was a witch, and a powerful one at that.

Magic rolled through her, swelling like an ocean wave as it swirled at her fingertips, ready to enact her command. Snow danced in spirals as her air and water magic mingled together, gleefully intertwining with the natural elements that always surrounded Alice. Magic swept from her, rushing to assess the man running toward them. Alice's magic spoke to her, and she recognized the familiar magical signature.

"It is alright," Alice said to her parents, lightly pushing Giles out of the way. "It is Thomas Bradbury."

"This cannot be good," Giles muttered. "If he is in this much of a rush, he must herald news."

Alice nodded stiffly. Intuition slammed into her like a punch to the gut. Thomas did indeed have news, and Alice knew in her bones it was about the witch hunts.

Huffing, Thomas skidded to a stop, nearly tumbling into the women as he slid over the icy ground. Giles caught him with a beefy hand on the shoulder.

"Alice." The older gentleman held a hand to his chest as he gasped for air. He must have sprinted from town without stopping to catch the Coreys. "They have arrested Sarah Good."

Alice's frown grew strained as she regarded the witches accompanying her. Giles scrubbed a hand over his face, as though he could brush off the dismay seizing his features.

Martha gasped in horror, her eyes darting to look at her daughter. "Sarah Good is no witch."

"That is not all, Martha. The girls... they have accused Sarah Osborne."

It was as though Alice's own lightning had struck her. She staggered back, pressing a hand to her heart. They arrested an actual witch. And no amount of magic could remedy this. Even if Alice could save Sarah and the others, it would not end these witch hunts.

Martha gasped, tears welling in her eyes. She wrapped her arms around her torso, but Giles swept his wife into an embrace, as if he could protect her with his physical body. Thomas shuffled his feet in the snow, ignoring how the water soaked into his worn and torn boots.

Perhaps Alice could alter Hathorne's and Corwin's memories. But what of the rest of the townsfolk? Uriel rewrote the people's memories when she left Alice with the Coreys, but Alice did not know practical magic. And there was no one to teach her. Even if she could, Alice did not think her magic would be effective on Hathorne…. There was something wrong about him. As though he were not human. And how was this all connected to the dark entity she fought in her Trials? And until Alice knew exactly what supernatural entity she faced, she could not win this war.

"This does not forebode well for us. Any of us."

"What do we do, Miss Alice?"

"I need to think." Alice's brow furrowed as the wind blew around her skirts, her first element caressing her skin lovingly as it sought to comfort her. Staring at the sun setting on the dusky horizon, the overcast sky diminishing the light, she muttered more to herself than to her companions. "What game are you playing, Hathorne?"

And so it begins, a melodious yet ominous, otherworldly voice spoke into Alice's mind. A voice she heard every day until she was three. Her mother was warning her. Darkness would not wait until her seventeenth birthday in autumn.

The Salem War was already here.

CHAPTER EIGHT

DARKNESS FALLS

Innocent until proven guilty.

That was how the land's government should operate.

Alice swung her axe again, splitting the massive log in two. As the man of the house, Giles normally chopped wood, but her parents were aging, and Alice was physically strong—a blessing that came with being the Nephilim of Earth—and she had a lot of anger to work out.

Unrestrained magic wafted off Alice, but she was not concerned. She had long since constructed wards—protective magical enchantments—around her own house, and since these blasted witch hunts began, she erected them around the Corey's estate. The wards included a glamour, a spell to cast a mirage to change appearance, which Alice used to conceal her magic use.

It had been little more than a month since Tituba's arrest, and she had yet to stand trial.

Alice slammed the axe down, splitting yet another massive log. No female human or witch could exert such physical force, but Alice was no mere mortal.

She did not know if the delay in Tituba's trial was good or bad. On one hand, the delay lengthened Tituba's life, but she lived in squalor in those dungeons, and Alice wondered what dark and nefarious deeds were occurring during this stretch of time. Why did Hathorne want to delay the trial?

Nothing good. And Alice worried this extension of time would foster fear and allow Hathorne and Corwin to manipulate the townspeople further.

Splitting another log, Alice rammed the axe into the tree trunk base, lodging the blade deep in the wood. Yanking on the handle, she failed to withdraw the axe. Exhaling a rough breath, Alice paused to wipe the sweat from her forehead with an apron.

Gasping, Alice's spine straightened as a shock of magic wound through her like a current.

As though she had summoned him with her thoughts alone, Alice turned to find Hathorne and Sheriff Corwin stalking up the drive to John Proctor's residence. Hathorne turned, meeting her eye as his lips pulled into a vile smirk.

What was he doing here?

Restraining her magic, Alice pulled her energy close to her body to prevent the humans from sensing it. But with a subtle turn of her wrist, she sent Spirit to call her mother and father from where they rested within their home.

Moments later, Giles and Martha stood with Alice, watching from afar as Hathorne knocked on Proctor's door.

Giles had never cared for John Proctor, who served as the Earth Representative on the once disbanded Athenian Council, and the neighbors were famous for their rough disputes over what seemed to be trivial things to Martha and Alice. But as Giles crossed his burly arms over his barrel chest, Alice got the distinct impression that even Giles did not wish this hell on Proctor.

For they all knew what was coming.

Yet Alice uselessly stared, unable to do a thing to save her people, as the sheriff attempted to chain Proctor in shackles.

John wrenched away from the men, shouting something that could not be heard. No, Alice commanded the wind not to carry his words. She did not want to witness the dark deed beyond what she watched.

Proctor fought, struggling futilely to evade the grasp of the men, but something unnatural infused Hathorne's aura as he caught John by the wrist. With his thumb and forefinger, he pressed against the appendage and snapped the bone, bringing Proctor to his knees in pain.

Startled, Alice leapt back.

No mortal possessed such strength. Not even Alice.

Corwin snapped the chains around Proctor's wrists, then hauled Proctor to his feet and dragged him down the dirt drive.

Before she could stop him, Giles stormed forward, charging for the three men. "What is going on here? Where are you taking him?" Giles roared.

Sharing a frightened look, Alice and Martha hurried after him, letting themselves appear meek and weak so Hathorne might overlook them. Alice did not want her parents to become his next targets.

"Ah, Giles Corey." Hathorne tipped his hat. "Good day to you, sir. I suppose it is best that you know first, before the others find out. Mr. Proctor here has been accused of witchcraft."

"By who?" Giles growled.

"Miss Mary Warren."

Not good. Unlike the other accusers who were mere children, Mary Warren was a woman of twenty, older than Alice. And the Proctors' housemaid. Her word held greater weight, and given her proximity to the Proctors, she could convince the humans in the town of his guilt. And Proctor had openly and loudly disagreed with Tituba's arrest, and the hysteria driving the witch hunts.

This was a calculated strike by the Putnams.

Since Tituba's arrest, they jumped on the witch hunts with a viciousness Alice had seen from few mortals—human or witch. They were cut throat and unfazed by the prospect of murdering those who stood in their way. And with every conviction, the estate of the convicted would be forfeited to the government... but Alice did not doubt that the seized estates would end up in the hands of the Putnams.

The Putnams would seize more land, more money, and more control of Salem. Their lust for wealth would be the demise of Salem.

And the feud between the Putnams and the Proctors was widespread knowledge. As the two wealthiest families—and both witches—in town, their power struggle was at last coming to an end. Because John Proctor was not low enough to use these blasted witch hunts for his purposes by sacrificing the lives of innocents.

"Now you listen here, Magistrate." Giles waggled a finger in his face. "I am no friend of Proctor's, but I have lived next to him for near forty years, and not once have I witnessed such evil acts from him."

"You can bring that up during his trial, Mr. Corey, but until then, he must be detained. We cannot risk the evil that could come about if these witches go unchecked. It would be literal hell on earth."

"I'll tell you what is hell on earth." Giles stepped forward, raising his arm to strike Hathorne, but Alice could not allow that to happen.

Leaping forward, she grasped Giles's arm with both hands, pulling on him. With her power, she could have toppled him, but she did not want to raise suspicion with the use of unnecessary force that a normal woman could not replicate. Instead, she tugged gently on him, pulling him away from the men.

"Come, Father," she spoke loud enough for the men to hear. Her wide eyes met Proctor's as she tried to communicate with a look, to tell him she would find a way to save him. Looking at her with hazel eyes, he nodded almost imperceptibly as his magic touched Alice's. She sent a tendril of magic out to caress his, trying to reassure him that her power would be enough to save him and the others. "We can do nothing for him now. Let us go and pray for the end of these witch hunts." Her hunter green eyes pierced into Hathorne as she said the last part, hoping he understood the message veiled by her words— end the witch hunts by ending Hathorne.

A spiteful smile curled Hathorne's lips, and Alice's stomach dropped as nausea rolled inside her.

They were next.

Alice stared at the straw-strewn, worn wooden floors of the courthouse. Benches stood in rows, crammed full with townsfolk, and Alice sat with the Coreys in the middle. At the front of the room, nine men sat behind a massive oak table, with Hathorne at the center.

The Court of Oyer and Terminer.

The panel of crooked judges was led by the worst humanity had to offer—Hathorne and Corwin. Corwin was a weaselly, pathetic human with a sick addiction to torture. Rumors abounded as to the devilish experiments he performed in his basement, but Alice had yet to find any proof. Though she knew she must deal with it eventually. However, Corwin was not the most corrupt.

Hathorne was the real problem. He was connected to the Darkness Alice fought in both her Fire and Earth Trials. He stank of the same rot and mildew as the shadow creature, but Alice was not sure if he and it were one and the same. All she knew was he colluded with evil.

Across from the table stood the penalty box, measuring no more than two feet by two feet, entrapping the accused. Wooden spindles stretched from the floor to a railing encircling the dark-skinned woman on all four sides.

Tituba spent half an hour of this hoax of a trial presenting a disheartened denial of witchcraft. But Tituba was not ignorant. She knew she would never be acquitted, and with that knowledge, combined with pressure from Hathorne and the other men, Tituba quickly changed her tune to a confession.

Alice had hung her head when Tituba admitted to being a witch. It was the beginning of the end, and they all knew it. War was on her doorstep, and Alice did not know how to fight it. She had not mastered her Spirit Trial yet. She had time until her seventeenth birthday, yet... the Salem War was here.

She did not want to attend this ridiculous trial in the first place, but every witch in Salem sat in attendance, putting on a show, so they might not be the next to be convicted of witchcraft.

"The Devil came to me and bid me serve him," Tituba recounted in awkward, clunky English, learned after she was stolen from her home in the Caribbean to serve the Parris family.

"Who tortured the girls?" Hathorne demanded with unconcealed delight in his eyes.

"The Devil, for all I know," Tituba muttered. Glaring at Hathorne, Tituba spun her tale, one involving unholy acts, witches, unnatural creatures, and a strange man with accomplices with supernatural powers who forced her to hurt the children. Throughout her story, she mentioned Sarah Good and Sarah Osborne—smart of Tituba since the other women were already imprisoned—and a handful of other names, which Hathorne and his Court dutifully recorded, no doubt to so they could be arrested next.

While Tituba told the story Hathorne undoubtedly twisted together, she shot a daggered glare at him, a defeated woman. A defeated woman who masterfully shared her story, compelling the audience with her gloriously persuasive tone.

Alice smashed her lips together in a tight line to keep from speaking against the injustice of it all. Tuning out Tituba as she cantered on about black dogs and red cats and other non-existent beings, Alice dug her fingernails sharply into her palms, hard enough to break the skin. An injustice based on the word of two young girls.

The word of a slave carried no weight, not even against the word of two children. For Tituba, it was easier to confess to the crime and twist it as though she were at the mercy of a powerful otherworldly being. It was the only way for Tituba to escape death. Especially by demonizing Sarah Osborne and Sarah Good, whose words would carry more weight.

She was selfish.

Not that Alice could find it within herself to blame Tituba. The desire to live was a survival instinct Alice understood well. After facing death in four Trials, Alice understood the need for self-preservation. Given the same position, Alice was not sure she would act any more righteous.

But she must.

Tituba's actions, even if out of self-preservation, would impact Salem and the world for centuries to come. Alice could sense the truth of it in her bones. Nausea slammed into her stomach, and she resisted the urge to vomit.

The choices Alice made impacted not just her life and the lives of the people closest to her, but the lives of every creature in this world. It was a heavy burden to bear, and many, like Tituba, failed to carry the load, but Alice was the Salem Witch. She was not made to break under pressure but rise to her calling.

This was what she was created for.

"I cannot believe this," Martha exclaimed as she trudged through the slush behind Alice, allowing Giles to help her through the wetness.

"I do not know which is worse—Tituba lying and condemning those other women or that these cowards are buying it."

Alice paused, turning to face her parents. With a twist of her wrist, she wrapped a bubble of air around them so the wind would not carry their words to unwanted ears.

"The consequences of Tituba's actions will compound with the actions of the other women."

Martha and Giles exchanged an uneasy glance. "What do you mean?"

"Sarah Osborne and Sarah Good have yet to stand trial, and while they have more status than a slave like Tituba, they have little protection against the lies of these ridiculous girls and the spectral evidence they supposedly report."

"You think they will concede to Hathorne's questioning." Giles spoke the words as a statement rather than a question.

Alice nodded stiffly. "By admitting to witchcraft, which we know is a lie, Tituba propelled these witch hunts, giving Hathorne the traction he needs to make more accusations against other women. And the other women are likely to offer more names in exchange for their lives. And so on and so on."

"Abigail Williams and Betty Parris." Martha named the two girls who initially accused Tituba of witchcraft. "They must be stopped."

"While I agree with you, these monstrous girls have no understanding of the consequence of their actions. But I fear Tituba set the precedent for these trials." Alice shook her head. "Her 'confession' supplied imagery of the Devil and his accomplices, painting a picture in the minds of these horrible men as to how the witch hunts will proceed. It is neither those girls nor Tituba whom we must focus on, but Hathorne."

"What about Corwin?" Giles rumbled.

"While he is a rodent, I am not inclined to believe he is the mastermind behind these events. Hathorne is our enemy, and a cunning one at that. We must tread carefully, or we shall find ourselves in dire straits."

It was mid-April, yet Alice could not get warm, even with her fire magic to raise her body temperature. Perhaps it was from the biting wind blowing through the Misery Islands as Alice practiced with her Spirit magic—manifested as golden lightning. A biting wind she had summoned as she spelled together a massive storm, as she always did, to hide the unnatural lightning she unleashed in the air.

Like always, Alice had slinked off to the islands in the dead of night, the blackness serving as the most practical cover to conceal her witchcraft. Witchcraft that these foolish humans could not hope to comprehend, for the witchcraft they accused others of was nothing but folly.

Alice laughed to herself. They would not know what to do with themselves if she revealed the true extent of her powers.

But it would do no good, only causing more damage as it convinced humans of the absolute existence of witches, and by extension, witches would be associated with the Devil. How ridiculous. Alice was no more in cahoots with the Devil than an apostle, for the blood of angels ran through her veins.

Another bolt of golden lightning sparked through the stormy night sky, then another, and another, each dancing through the thunderous storm, the light refracting off the clouds.

Lightning. That was the form of Spirit. It was life-giving, yet, at the same time, it could take life as easily as it gave it. But Spirit was so much *more* than a bolt of lightning. Alice could not have described it if she tried. It was an element, but different. *More.* More than the elements themselves. It was the entity that created and sustained life. It was the power of the Creator, and that a mortal like Alice was granted access... it was still somewhat unbelievable to her.

Alice gazed at the moon overhead, charting its course through the night sky. It was growing late... or early. Dawn was not long off, the sky lightening to a charcoal gray. She should return home.

Not that her parents would worry—Martha and Giles were fully aware of her nightly endeavors, even if they discontinued their own practice like the rest of the witches in Salem. Since Tituba's arrest, Alice was the only practicing witch, the others too scared to use their magic for fear of discovery.

She understood their fears.

Alice would not allow fear to dictate her actions and declare who she was or was not. She was a witch, and she intended to live like one, whether she was confined to the shadows or not.

As the Salem Witch, she could not afford to be passive in her training. Her birthday was not long off, and with tensions rising in Salem, it was only a matter of time before Alice called upon Spirit to save the world.

She just did not know *how*.

Glancing at the moon one last time, Alice sent a prayer to the Heavens, begging her mother to show her the way.

Summoning the power swirling in her core, Alice wrapped green light around her body, willing it to spirit her across space in the blink of an eye.

Her feet slammed into the worn floorboards of her parents' home. Ever since John Proctor's arrest, Alice had returned to living with Martha and Giles at their insistence. It was unwise for a single woman, even a widow, to live alone during these treacherous times. It would be too easy for one of those ludicrous children to accuse a lone woman of witchcraft, especially one as strong and full of vitality as Alice.

Stillness and silence greeted her inside the house.

Alice froze in place. She did not sense her parents' magical signatures. But she did sense a Darkness, an indigo stain lingering in the house.

She ran to her parents' bedroom, flinging the door open.

Their bed lay empty, the covers thrown carelessly back. Martha would never leave her house in such upheaval. And that darkness... it permeated the room, its stench of death and rot and mildew suffocating the air Alice tried to breathe.

No, that was her chest. It was too tight, constricting too much for her to inhale. Or maybe she could not exhale.

Her knees slammed into the floorboards, and she wept. Sobs wracked her body as tears fell to the ground in rivers, a small puddle forming. Falling forward, Alice crumpled into a ball in the doorway as she gasped for breath.

Giles and Martha had been arrested for witchcraft.

And Alice was next.

Magic zinged through Alice, her wards alerting her to the presence of a dark, malicious being. A being who had haunted her for months now, if not years.

Dropping the knife she held for chopping vegetables, Alice wiped her hands on the white apron hanging from her waist, then bowed her head and prayed to her Creator.

She could spook, flee from this place, find Ariel, and never return to this hell of Hathorne's. After their arrest, her parents had bid her to do such, to find Elizabeth Bradbury and raise her daughter. But they forgot, if Alice reached her seventeenth birthday without passing her Spirit Trial, she forfeited her life. Today was the twelfth of May, leaving Alice with four months to trigger her final Trial.

It was not only that thought that bound Alice to Salem. She was the Nephilim of Earth, the chosen champion of Heaven. The Salem Witch did not run from evil but ran toward it with the power of the five elements at her beck and call. Too many lives were at stake. Alice would not run, so she hit her knees and bowed her head, praying to her Creator for strength for what was to come.

First Proctor, then Giles and Martha. Hathorne arrested them for no reason other than to set the precedent for him to accuse Alice of witchcraft without question. For Giles had questioned Proctor's arrest, as did others. But arresting a whole family... Hathorne had expertly planned this from the beginning, possibly since before Tituba's arrest. It had never been about witches. It had always been about *her*. About Alice and the threat she posed.

Hathorne knew. He knew she was the Salem Witch.

She did not know how, but she knew he was linked to the Prince of Hell that had attacked her twice now.

A sharp rap sounded against the door, and Alice rose to her feet, straightened her spine and threw her shoulders back.

Unflinchingly, she strode to the door and opened it to reveal Magistrate Hathorne leering at her from the doorstep, flanked on either side by Reverend Corwin and Sheriff Corwin, the propagators of the Salem Witch Trials.

At last, they had come for her.

Alice's fiery red hair swayed around her waist with each subtle movement, falling in unkept waves, dirt and mud caked into the strands. Dirt clung to her wool dress from sleeping on the floor of her prison cell.

Disheveled as she may look, Alice faced the Court of Oyer and Terminer with unwavering calm.

Hathorne grinned vindictively over his papers at Alice, his eyes flashing indigo. Shock slapped Alice across the face, then quickly hardened to stone.

When a human was possessed by a demon, their eyes turned red, but when a mortal channeled the powers of a demon, their eyes turned completely black.... But for Hathorne's eyes to be indigo... the same color as that dark entity...

He was the enemy—he was the Sin, the Prince of Hell.

It had been Hathorne that night at the church. The night she destroyed the army of demons and passed her Fire Trial. It was him the night her daughter was born. Hathorne was her enemy all along. She should have assassinated him in his sleep. But it was not that simple. He was a demon. A Prince of Hell who possessed the power of one of the Seven Deadly Sins. But which one?

"Ahem," Hathorne cleared his throat, drawing this out to torture Alice. "Miss... Ah, no, Mrs. Alice Parker, also known as Goody Parker. You are the wife of John Parker, the mariner?"

Alice nodded tersely and kept her response short. "I am."

She would not play his game. She would not speak more than necessary. Speaking could get away from one, and that was how one ended up dead.

Hathorne frowned at her, displeasure written across his face at her refusal to play by his rules.

"Mrs. Parker, Mary Warren charges you with several acts of witchcraft. What say you in response? Are you guilty or not?" He nearly hissed the word "guilty" at her.

Her response did not matter. The malicious energy wafting off his body, infused in his aura, told Alice everything about his desires. He wanted to see her hang, more so than any other woman accused in these accursed trials.

But why?

She was not wealthy. She did not hold power with the government or the church, nor did she attempt to steal wealth or power from the Putnams, who used these witch hunts to their advantage by accusing those who stood in their way to more wealth and social status. But they were witches, and they knew her identity.

Betrayed by the very witches she sought to save.

Then Alice realized potency of the fury mixed with power radiating off her. No witch possessed such considerable raw magic flowing through their veins. She was a force to be reckoned with, and the Putnams recognized her potential to usurp them with not only her magic, but her status as the Reigning Salem Witch. And they rightfully feared it.

Hathorne knew it too, but his motivation for ridding her from this world differed from the Putnams', but they gave him the power he needed to end her. Different reasons, same objective.

And she and her family spoke against the trials from the beginning, even defending Tituba, a slave. But some people had listened enough for Alice to convince them Tituba was human and these trials were not about witches. Why else would the girls accuse a slave, someone without status? Because she was an easy target.

The Putnams and Hathorne knew most of the town would stand idly by or actively participate in convicting Tituba. She was merely a tool to them, an outsider they could use to instigate the trials and gain traction for the witch hunts on their terms.

Alice's stomach rolled, and she fought the urge to vomit the bile filling her mouth. Her intuition. She was right. About all of it.

Hathorne knew she possessed the power to rid him from this world. Did he know she was the Salem Witch?

Evil. This was evil conducted by the hands of demons. No, not demons. Perhaps Hathorne was steeped in darkness, but the

Putnams were mortals. Alice would not dehumanize these horrific actions. It was their humanity that made their actions so terrifying.

"I am not guilty," she answered simply.

"You told her you cast away Thomas Westgate." Hathorne challenged her.

"I know nothing of it."

Hathorne's agitation heightened with each response. "You told her John Lapthorn was lost to the spectral lands. How do you plea against this spectral evidence?"

"I never spoke a word to her in my life." Alice spoke adamantly, not a trace of nervousness or submissiveness on her face or in her voice. If she showed the faintest amount of weakness, Hathorne would devour her.

"You told her you bewitched her sister," Hathorne accused. "Because her father would not mow your grass."

"I never saw her." Alice's simple answers drove Hathorne up the wall, and he bristled, his eyes flashing indigo.

"Your Honor." A young girl, no older than twenty, jumped to her feet.

When Hathorne waved at her to speak, she asked, "May I strike the accused? I believe you shall receive proof to convict her of being a witch."

"You may proceed," Hathorne agreed, an evil smile twisting his lips as he leaned back in his chair and watched Alice over steepled hands.

Warren strode confidently from her pew toward Alice, who schooled her face to remain neutral as the young woman approached. Warren was not within three feet of the penalty box when she tumbled backward, her back hitting the floor as she convulsed in a violent fit. Her body seized and contorted unnaturally as she cried out in pain. Her arms and legs twisted as her body thrashed against the wooden floor as she writhed in fabricated agony.

Anybody with half a brain could see she was faking it. That is what the Plymouth Colony Salem Witch Trials were—a group of pathetic girls crawling their way to power by cutting down the other women of their town. Not just cutting down, but guaranteeing their execution. They were nothing more than murders, tools that Hathorne and Putnam leveraged for their perverted agendas.

Two men rushed forward, grabbing the seizing girl by her arms and dragging her away from Alice. Once pulled to the opposite side of the room, her fit abruptly stopped and she crawled to her feet, a triumphant expression on her face.

She thrust a finger at Alice and spoke to the room, "See! Did you not witness Goody performing witchcraft on me before your very eyes?"

The hall burst with noise as neighbor turned to neighbor, speaking hushed murmurs to one another. Some cast fearful glances at Alice, others surveyed the hall nervously, as though they could spot a witch on sight alone, but at least half the hall had mixed expressions of disbelief, skepticism, and downright anger, though those were mostly the real witches.

The Court of Oyer and Terminer used nothing more than spectral evidence to condemn the women who were accused before Alice, and she knew it would be no different for her. It was illogical, lacking all scientific reasoning, but that was the point. It was how Hathorne manipulated the situation to get what he coveted—a noose around Alice's neck.

A man leapt to his feet, shouting, "This is ridiculous. You cannot take this child's actions as evidence. It is not evidence at all—merely a child playing pretend."

Others in the hall muttered their agreements but were quickly cut off by Magistrate Jonathon Corwin when he slammed his fist on the table, hissing at the observers, "Silence." The crowd fell into a disgruntled quiet, allowing the trial to resume.

"Mary Warren, are you ready to give your deposition in front of the Court of Oyer and Terminer?" Hathorne asked her, an eager glint in his eye.

"I am." She nodded, then strode to the witness stand. She placed her right hand on the Holy Bible and raised her left hand, palm facing out, as she swore to tell the truth or so help her God. Sitting, the cunning serpent spun her story. "Goody Parker told me she has been a witch these twelve years and then some. Ann Pudeator told me she hurt James Coyes's child, taking him from his mother's hands," Mary insisted.

"Is there anything else?" Hathorne urged the girl.

With a glance of feigned nervousness at Alice, she nodded.

Alice resisted the temptation to light Mary on fire with holy flames as justice for breaking the oath she swore with her hand on the holy tomb.

"Do not be afraid, Mary. If you tell us the truth, we will protect you from any, ah, evildoing afoot."

Alice wanted to scream. This man, who was not a man, was the evildoer. He was the demon perpetuating these horrors.

Swallowing roughly, the girl piped up the courage to speak. "Parker brought me a poppet of Mercy—Mercy Lewis—and told me how to use it—to hurt Mercy. But I did not ask her to, I swear. I did not hurt Mercy. It was her," she exclaimed, thrusting her finger in Alice's direction, who appeared utterly unperturbed.

Alice had to hand it to her—her theatrics were astoundingly good. She belonged on stage at the Globe Theatre. Alice wanted nothing more than to wring her lying little throat.

"When I refused her, she turned on me, piercing the poppet with a needle to its heart, thereby afflicting me." Mary burst into a fit, her head flew backward, and her limbs convulsed in jerky, awkward movements. Her tongue lolled out of her mouth and drool ran down her cheek, but that was not what made the courtroom gasp—Mary's tongue was black.

Mutterings erupted throughout the room as humans believed the discoloration of her tongue to be proof of witchcraft, but the true witches knew what it meant—black magic had been cast upon Mary.

Alice did not know to what end, but this confirmed her suspicions of the Sin casting its evil throughout the town.

But for what purpose?

When Mary composed herself, she cast a blatant glare at Alice. "See there, these fits of mine are caused by Goody. She has bewitched me with her evil craft. Not only that, but she murdered my mother."

"Please elaborate, Miss Warren," Corwin insisted.

"Not long after Goody visited our home, did my sister and mother take ill. Soon after the illness took hold—a strange unnatural one— did my mother pass."

"Was this before or after she came to you with the poppet?" Another Court judge inquired.

"Before." She frowned. "No, after? I am not sure." She chewed her bottom lip uncertainly. "Now, I am not quite certain. It must be... she... she is responsible. She is using her witchcraft on me, altering my memories so she might escape the consequences of her sins." Mary burst into another fit, shaking and convulsing. This fit did not last as long as the first, probably as she grew tired of her charade.

When she recovered, Hathorne encouraged her, "Was there anything else, Miss Warren?"

"Yes, Magistrate." She nodded eagerly. "When Goody brought the poppet to me, she told me of a Bloody Sacrament, a meeting with the Devil, attended by her and some other thirty witches." Mary convulsed, the fit lasting no longer than thirty seconds. "See, her magic is weakened as she uses it. She has afflicted me now several times, each one less terrible than the one before as her craft grows weaker."

"This is preposterous." William Proctor jumped to his feet. "This *girl* is fabricating fantastical stories, fantastical stories that *never* happened. My father saw the truth of this, and he saw through the façade and openly spoke out against this ridiculous witch hysteria. When father gave this girl, his servant, more chores to keep her busy, she did not accuse a single soul of devilry. Until she accused my father and mother, and you believe she did not intentionally choose the two people keeping her from her glorious status as an accuser?"

John Proctor had been arrested on charges of witchcraft shortly before Alice's father and mother. Giles, who despised Proctor as a neighbor, spoke against the preposterousness of the accusation. Eight days later, Giles was in custody. It would not be long before Hathorne arrested William for speaking out against the hysteria.

"Look, William." Reverend Noyes frowned at him. "I understand you are upset about your parents, but this woman—"

"This woman's name is Alice. And she consorts with the Devil no more than you do, Reverend. She is a good and honest woman. She is pious to the point that we nicknamed her *Goody*. You may allow the wool to be pulled over your eyes, but like my mother and father, I see these trials for what they are—a ploy for power by the Putnams."

A collective gasp sounded through the hall, followed by outbursts of chatter amongst the townsfolk. Men and women stood, shouting their support of William. Others frowned, glancing between William and Alice, considering his words regarding the matter. Despite having the support of the people, it mattered little for Alice, and William likely condemned himself by defending her.

Alice's eyes fluttered shut. Oh, William... what did you do to yourself?

"Silence," Hathorne bellowed, smashing his gavel against the wooden table. The room fell into an abrupt but uneasy silence. "Now," Hathorne continued, an indignant and irritated expression souring his face, "the Court of Oyer and Terminer calls Thomas Westgate to the stand."

An ugly, unwashed man in his forties, rose from his pew and made his way to the witness stand. Placing his right hand on a Bible, he gave his oath to tell the truth. Taking his seat, he looked at Hathorne.

"Thomas Westgate, you have been called to court to provide a deposition regarding witchcraft performed by Alice Parker. What evidence do you place before the court?"

Westgate smiled vindictively, revealing several missing teeth, and the others were rotting away from the black plaque rimming the gums. Alice swallowed the bile that rose in her throat from revulsion.

"I ain't see Goody much, but not some mont's ago, she come in ter our company at da tavern. She came ter scold her husband, callin' him ter come home. I took her husban's part, tellin' her it be unbeseeming for her ter come after him in da tavern ter rail him like dat. With dem words, she came up ter me, and she had da nerve ter call me a 'rogue' an' bid me ter min' me business, then she tol' me I been better tif I ain't say nothin'."

Hathorne frowned. "Mr. Westgate, while your testimony is revealing of the character of the accused, it does not implicate her of witchcraft."

"Jus' hol' on der, woncha? Ders more ter da story. Twas later dat nigh' I be frighten' awful bad. I be going from da house of Daniel King, when I stumble ore ter John Robinson's, and I hear a thundrin' noise... and ter it was. A black hog runnin' towar' me with its mouth wide open, like he gonn' devour me. I be migh'y afraid, an' I try ter run from da beast, but I wen' tumblin' ta da groun'. I fell on me hip, and me knife run in ter my hip, all da way up ter the shaft. When I ge' up, me stocking an' shoe be full wit blood, so I had ter crawl 'long the fence til I made it ter me home. All da while, dat damn hog stalkin' me. Ain't leave me alone, he ain't. When I stumble ter da door, da knife ain't in me hip no more. Twas in da sheath. An' I drew et, the sheath fell ter pieces."

"And what did you make of this strange hog, Mr. Westgate?" Hathorne grinned victoriously.

"Dat hog eith'r the Devil or some othe' evil thing. It wain't no hog. Ain't no doubt in me min' it twas Goody Parker, or by her means, she call da beast with dat evil witchcraft of hers."

Hathorne reclined in his chair with a triumphant smile. Alice kept her expression neutral, refusing to give into despair despite the mutterings of the room, which suggested those present either thought her to be a witch, or feared the testimony was enough to condemn her as such.

"Thank you, Mr. Westgate." Hathorne smiled knowingly at Westgate. "Is there anything else you would like to say before you leave the stand?"

But Alice knew it would not end with Westgate. During her astral adventures and midnight plots, she found Hathorne's list of witnesses—Margaret Jacobs, Marshal Herrick, Thomas Putnam, and Reverend Noyes, who was clearly in cahoots with Hathorne—would testify against her.

"Aye, sir. I tink ever'one ter know, Goody Parker, der ain't no doubt in me min' dat she a witch, a witch dat be colludin' wit der Devil, a'right. Ain't nothin' more ter it."

Alice remained stoic in the face of the blatant accusation, but her fellow witches looked on in fear. Several of the other witches in the hall sobbed as they began to understand this witch hunt had nothing to do with finding actual witches. It was a ploy for power, and the Putnams would walk over anyone and everyone to grab hold of it.

But the Putnams were not the problem, and only Alice knew the truth as she glared at Hathorne.

He was a Prince of Hell. She was sure of it, and after observing him, she knew who he was.

He was Asmodeus, the Sin of Lust.

CHAPTER NINE

I Hate Dungeons

Alice's specter stood under a blazing summer sun. She snorted to herself. Here she was, the spectral evidence Hathorne and the rest of the Court so loved to use against their victims, yet not a soul was aware of her presence.

She was astral projecting—projecting her spirit out of her body to move freely and invisibly on the earthly plane—from the prison cell she shared with her mother and father.

The oppressive heat beat down on the profusely sweating townspeople. Their thick wool pants and dresses only intensified the sweltering heat. Yet, despite the heat, a crowd gathered around the wooden platform with a single beam running overhead, a rope tied to the beam on one end, a noose knotted on the other.

A scream pierced the air.

Alice spun around to find Sarah Good, who she had watched in person be dragged from the dungeon mere minutes ago, being wrenched down the dirt path by Reverend Noyes—who was as much of a monster as Corwin and Hathorne, delighting in the sick perversion that were the trials—as he pulled her by her rope-bound hands to where Hathorne and Corwin stood on the gallows.

Sarah struggled vehemently against Noyes, pulling against her restraints, biting and kicking at the man holding her prisoner.

Despite her small stature, Sarah fought with every fiber of her being as the vile man pulled her toward a death she could already see. By the time Noyes wrestled her onto the stage and tightened the noose around her neck, he looked worse for wear than the woman he was about to hang.

Sarah glared with unfathomable rage and hatred, daring Noyes to come and get a piece of her.

Alice approached the foot of the gallows, staring at Sarah with regret. Sarah was not one of her people, but she was a good woman and a child of the Creator. And Alice had failed to save her. Even if she had freed Sarah from her prison, she had nowhere to go, and she could only run from Hathorne and the witch hunts for so long. And Alice would only condemn herself by revealing her magic to a human.

A man behind Alice whispered to his companion, "First Bridget, now Sarah. As if either woman has done anything to harm Salem."

Swallowing, Alice forced down the grief threatening to rise in her throat. Bridget was the first to fall, the first victim of these horrid trials. Alice had not astral projected then, for she did not know Bridget was to be hanged. When the jailers came to seize her from the dungeons, Alice thought... they all thought it was for another deposition, not a hanging. Bridget had been a beloved companion.... No, Alice would not think about her now, lest her grief get the better of her when she needed a clear head.

"Hush, William," his female companion warned. "Your parents have been accused. I do not wish for you to be next."

"You and I both know the people accused are either outcasts, so these serpents can seize their estates, or those who pose a hindrance to Putnam's grab for power," the man countered. "I have already defied Hathorne and these absurd trials. If I am to hang, my fate is already sealed."

It was a miracle that William hadn't been arrested yet...

"Yes." The woman hissed a breath out through her teeth. "But that does not mean we should discuss this here, of all places."

Alice tuned out the rest of their conversation, letting it fall into the background noise of the crowd's conversations, unable to listen to another word that reminded her of her fallen friend.

The town was split. Half of the gathered crowd eagerly awaited Sarah's execution. The other half dreaded it, futilely hoping Sarah would be miraculously spared.

"Sarah Good," Noyes announced. "You are accused and convicted of being a witch and a servant of the Devil. You are sentenced to death for your crimes against humanity. Last opportunity—do you confess your crimes and repent in front of man and God?"

Sarah spat at Noyes. She was too far away to hit him, but the mere gesture infuriated him. If she was to die, she would die defiantly, unlike Tituba, who caved to the pressure and escaped death.

"The decorum." He gasped, aghast at her actions. "Only a witch would deign to spit on a servant of the Lord. You are a witch in life, and in death, you will suffer in Hell as is befitting of a witch."

"You are a liar!" Sarah screamed at Noyes. The sweat brought on by the sweltering summer day dripped down her face, mixing with the streams of tears rushing from her eyes. "I am no more a witch than you are a wizard, and if you take away my life, God will give you blood to drink."

A shiver wracked through Alice's physical body as her stomach rolled. Witch or not, Sarah's words were a curse, and Alice knew in her soul that Death would execute the woman's hex. Words held great power—they held the ability to inflict great damage or heal the deepest wounds—and all words were spells, whether humans and witches intended it or not.

Noyes smiled sinisterly at Sarah as he pulled the lever. The boards beneath her clunked down, and the rope twanged as the noose around her neck caught, snapping the bone instantly.

Cheers rang from the crowd, mixed with horrified gasps.

Bile rose in Alice's throat as dark green light clouded her vision, whisking away the image of Sarah's body swinging from the gallows as Alice's spirit slammed into her body.

Falling to her side, Alice vomited in the dirt.

"Mother, if you are listening," Alice looked at the ceiling of her cell, her eyes unfocused as if she could see through the building above her and to the Heavens above, "I beg you, hear Sarah's prayer and send Death to drown Noyes in his own blood. May he suffer in this life and the next."

Alice spat, cleaning the taste of bile from her mouth, and clamored to her feet.

"What is it?" Martha asked from where she lay cradled in Giles's arms. "Alice, what did you see?"

Alice strode to the prison bars caging her in and wrapped her hands around the metal. She could rip the metal apart with a mere thought. Metal was a derivative of the earth, and the earth was hers to command.

But she could not run away from this war. Not when so many lives depended on her. She had to find a way to fight. Even locked in this cell, she would find a way to spare as many as possible. She would fight the Darkness threatening to consume these lands.

"Brace yourselves," Alice warned. "They hanged Sarah Good. And her death is just the beginning. This is not the end. I saw the people. The townsfolk who support the hunts were fanatical about her execution. The other half are too afraid to speak out against this new way of life." Alice spat through the bars. "They will sit idly by during these dark times, because if someone else is hanged, then at least it is not them."

"As if that will protect them," Giles said, drawing Martha closer.

"Mortals have always been strange in that they do exactly the thing they know they should not. Even when they know better, they choose the very things that are destructive to them."

Alice stared at the floor outside her cell, her thoughts churning inside her mind as she devised a plan.

"I have an idea."

Alice could spook, an ability only the most powerful of witches could muster, and Alice was nothing if not powerful. So, escaping the dungeon was easy. A flash of green later, and Alice stood wherever she pictured in her mind's eye.

And tonight, she stood outside of Reverend Jonathon Corwin's house.

Rumors were that Corwin performed unspeakable experiments—crimes against humanity—in his basement. Experiments that would end tonight.

With a snap of her fingers, Alice conjured her wand in a flash of green. Carved vines wound along the length of the wand to the handle with the emerald embedded in its base.

Wordlessly, Alice raised the wand overhead. The emerald glowed as she cast a spell, the magic of the glamour dripping onto her head and rolling down her body like raindrops falling on her.

Not even her shadow was visible to the mortal eye. Alice had cloaked herself, for she could not be seen for what she was about to do.

Quiet as a mouse, Alice slipped inside Corwin's house, easing the door shut so she did not make a sound.

Silent and invisible.

Stepping inside the dark house, Alice let her magical senses extend rather than relying on her physical ones. Nothing alive resided in the house—except rodents and vermin, including the weaselly cockroach hiding in the basement.

Seems the rumors held a kernel of truth.

Fearlessly, Alice let the green light of her magic flow from her, illuminating the darkened corridor. There, in the corner of the hallway, the slots between the floor planks sucked her light into the hollow space below. She should have known based on the stench of rot and mold wafting from that direction.

Creeping for the door, Alice swiped a hand through the air, gently lifting the door to the cellar so she could ease herself into the hole in the floor before letting the door shut quietly behind her.

Harsh blue light flickered from torches below.

Hellfire.

Hathorne must have summoned the perpetually burning fire for Corwin. Alice had long suspected Corwin was wicked but mortal, but Hathorne...

Swiftly, Alice descended the rickety stairs, her footfalls barely touching the worn wooden planks with the help of her air magic. Not a squeak sounded from her as she reached the bottom step.

Alice stood pressed between the narrow stairwell and the rough earthen wall of the cellar, lined with sturdy wood posts to keep the earth from caving into the basement. Whoever built this cellar crafted it with the intent for it to last a long time. And while some homes in Salem were built with care to endure the long winters, few were constructed with such a structure as this cellar. Because this cellar was meant to conceal the dark deeds of Corwin's nighttime activities.

A groan sounded from around the corner.

Activities that Corwin currently engaged in.

Invisible, Alice shuffled sideways to squeeze between the side of the staircase and the wall. Turning the corner, Alice swallowed the gasp that threatened to escape her at the sight.

Strapped to a gurney with leather restraints, laid a woman on the brink of death. Lacerations covered her from head to toe, the edges of the open wounds tinged with infection and her skin discolored by black and purple bruises—both on display around the rags, covering her body. Tubes and beakers and glass jars containing various colored liquids were assembled on a massive plank table on the other side of the woman, some bubbling, others misting, and more glowing.

Corwin stood with his back to Alice, grumbling to himself as he worked over another table, scribbling in a thick tome, probably filled with years of notes. Against the wall was erected a bookshelf, filled with other tomes. Decades of notes from Corwin's experiments. Experiments on women like the one held captive now.

With a grumble, Corwin turned from the table to stare at the woman, malicious calculation in his eyes. His beady little eyes shot to a vial sitting on a pedestal above the rest. With a virulent grin, Corwin palmed the vial and blundered around the table to the woman's side, hovering above her as he connected the vial to a tube with a needle at the end.

The woman's eyes shot open.

Alice took a startled step back, her spine pressing into the wall of the cellar.

Piercing the needle into the skin of the woman's arm, Corwin tipped the vial upside down, so the swirling indigo liquid slid down the tube.

The veins on the woman turned black as the devilish liquid pumped into her body, spreading rapidly. The skin around the puncture turned a dark blue, and the woman's body convulsed.

Corwin swore, ripping out the needle just long enough for her contractions to cease. Sinking the needle into her other arm, he emptied the second half of the vial into her veins.

A whimper escaped the woman's lips, followed by a severe backhand from Corwin as he hissed at her for silence.

All the while, Alice stood against the wall of the cellar, staring in paralyzed horror at the evil in her midst.

An evil that would end. Tonight.

And it would not go unpunished.

Fierce magic raged from Alice, shooting into the house above her head. Letting her green magic work of its own accord, Alice unleashed her power, trashing Corwin's house above. It was not enough, not nearly enough compared to what Alice wanted to do to the soulless human.

But it caused a startling commotion.

Corwin jumped away from the woman, as his eyes narrowed at the floorboards above their heads. Corwin scuttled down the narrow passage toward the staircase. Pressing herself flat against the wall, Alice held her breath, praying Corwin did not sense her. Since he was not supernatural like Hathorne, Corwin was oblivious to the sheer magic flowing off Alice unceasingly.

Corwin disappeared up the staircase, and Alice pressed the tip of her wand to the top of her head, the embedded emerald glowing with light. Magic dripped over her from head to toe, revealing herself to the woman, who did not so much as flinch at her sudden appearance. With brokenness in her eyes, the woman's head swiveled to Alice.

"I am going to free you from this hell." Alice reached for the woman's bindings.

"No," she croaked.

Alice froze with her hand hovering over the woman, staring wide-eyed at the woman. "Wh-what? You wish to remain here?"

"No." The woman shook her head, tears welling in her eyes. "I have listened to his mad mutterings. The liquid he injected into me… it is a substance made of the darkest kind of magic. In a few hours, it will transform me into something unrecognizable. A creature of darkness, and my soul will be stuck in the abyss."

"He is turning you into a demon?" Alice asked, aghast. "Why?"

"I do not know the reason. But he speaks of a growing evil and that he will be the one to create the dark creatures who spread Lust through the realm."

"A succubus," Alice said with sudden realization. A demon of seduction. "Have you felt any stirrings? A power in your loins?" Alice asked hesitantly, not wanting to pry, but needing to know Corwin's goal.

Hot tears ran in rivers down the woman's cheeks as she nodded. "It is too late for me. I have been here for weeks, undergoing his ministrations. I am not the first he has experimented on, but you must ensure I am the last."

Grasping the woman's hand with a fierce grip, Alice promised, "I will."

Sucking in a rattling breath, the woman closed her eyes before snapping them open. "In a few hours, his evil will root into my soul, and I will be lost. But not if you end me first. Kill me, so I may be free."

"But—"

"If you do not, my immortal soul will be doomed. And I do not wish to be trapped forever. Please, release me so I may return to the Garden and into the waiting arms of our Lord and Lady."

"I have never taken a life," Alice spoke softly. "Perhaps I can save you with the power of Spirit?"

"Perhaps, but there is not time for you to try. Corwin will return shortly, and then it will be too late. Please," the woman begged, pleading in her eyes. "Use your lightning to end me. Quickly."

"Spirit is not meant to kill. It is life-giving," Alice argued. She would find a way. Another way.

"It is both, dear child," the woman said sagely. "It can take as easily as it gives, like our Creator. You must be willing to use it for both purposes if you are to truly understand Its essence and master your final element, Salem Witch."

Alice did not know what to say. So, with tears in her eyes, she raised her hands and pressed them to the bare skin on the woman's chest.

Meeting Alice's hunter green gaze, the woman nodded, resolve in her eyes.

"May you rest in peace within the Garden."

Golden lightning crackled from Alice's hands, electrocuting the woman in a sudden shock.

And then she was gone.

Painless. Alice made it painless, but the loss of life...

Alice's knees slammed into the dirt as she wrapped her arms around her torso. Hot tears rolled down her cheeks as she rocked herself back and forth.

What was wrong with her? How could Alice have killed the woman without so much as trying to save her with the power of Spirit? It was the woman's wish, but... did that make it right? Alice was Nephilim, but for the first time, she realized that her soul may not be as clean as she once thought it to be.

Her soul is at rest with the angels, Uriel said to Alice, quieting her sobs. *Forgive yourself and rise, for your work is not done.*

With an anguished nod, Alice rose to her feet, but she did not try to stop the tears pouring from her eyes. Snapping her fingers, Alice spooked the woman's corpse in a flash of green light so she could ensure a proper burial later.

Dirt rained on Alice as Corwin blundered about overhead. He would be busy straightening the house for a while—Alice's magic left nothing untouched, giving her time for her magic to do its work down here.

She did not need long.

Air wrapped around the basement, forming a sound barrier, so Corwin did not hear the racket she was about to make.

A cyclone of air ripped out of her, swirling around the basement in a rage, knocking over the vials of vile liquids and potions and brews, smashing the glasses, and destroying equipment. Air wrenched the tables and gurneys from the ground and threw them against the earthen walls. Metal tools blew around Alice on the air currents, but she ruined those with a shot of earth magic.

Green flames leapt from her hands in a torrent, devouring the shelves of journals. Alice watched with a certain vindictive satisfaction as Corwin's years of notes burned. She did not tear her eyes away from her flames until nothing remained but ash. Whatever demented knowledge he gained through the dark arts was now lost, hopefully forever.

At her mental command, water swelled from under the earth, rising into the basement. More and more puddled around her, until Alice stood ankle-deep in murky green water, but she did not stop the flow of magic flooding the evil laboratory as she called upon her beloved element.

Thrusting her hands at the hard-packed earth under her feet, Alice curled her fingers. Green magic sank into the ground, burrowing deep under the earth to find the plant life underground. Yanking it to the surface, Alice willed her magic to grow the plants rapidly, aging them from seedlings to adults—poisonous plants that released deadly toxins into the air. The blossoms sprang open, releasing their pollutants into the air.

As the Nephilim of Earth, the plants' toxins did not dare to harm her, but Corwin, even if granted supernatural powers by Hathorne, could not enter the basement without suffering a slow, painful death for as long as Alice's magic lingered here. This cellar would never again house his evil experiments.

Dark green light swallowed Alice, and she spooked, leaving behind that horrid basement to re-materialize in the desolate graveyard behind the church of Salem. Mist crept through the burial site, shrouding Alice and the unnamed woman's body in its fog, hiding them from view.

Good. Alice could use the cover for what she was about to do, even if it was the witching hour and humans were unlikely to be roaming about.

Palm facing up, Alice raised her hand, the motion commanding her magic to scoop six feet worth of dirt from an empty plot and dump it on the side of the grave. Another wave of her hand lifted the woman's body on a gust of air to ease her into the hole in the ground, laying her to rest.

Speaking in tongues, Alice muttered under her breath before praying over the woman's body, blessing her body and soul, which had already entered the Garden.

Staring at the woman's broken body, Alice wondered if she could have used the power of Spirit to reverse the dark magic Corwin pumped into the nameless woman's body. Perhaps... perhaps Alice could have saved a life instead of taken one. She was *Nephilim*. What Nephilim took a life?

A Nephilim who wishes to show mercy on a soul, her mother's voice whispered through her mind, and peace washed over Alice. It had been a mercy to the woman. But her death would weigh heavily on Alice's soul. As would all the deaths of the Salem Witch Trials.

Glancing at the woman one last time, Alice waved her hand, shoveling the dirt into the grave in a single motion. Another flourish of her wrist and a block of stone emerged from the earth at the top of the grave. Waving her hand through the air, Alice etched a single word across the top of the headstone—Unknown. Underneath, she scribbled the words "The last woman to conquer the evil in the basement".

Alice did not know the woman's identity. She could not find the woman's family and give them closure, but she could honor the woman's death, since she was the one who doled it out.

Death was a burden Alice would endure forever.

With a sigh and a flash of dark green light, Alice spooked, returning to the cell she shared with her parents in the underground dungeon.

Glancing at where her parents lay curled around one another in the dirt, Alice lowered herself to the ground, finding some relief in the contact with her beloved element.

Rolling to her side, she turned her back on her parents, letting her mind wander to a time when she had been happy, however brief a time that had been when she was married and her husband was alive.

Alice did not know if she would ever be happy again, but she would not stop fighting to create a future for the ones she loved to find their happiness. And with that thought, Alice drifted to sleep, where she dreamed of the Darkness and trials and demons that she knew she would wake to in the morning.

For her final trial before the Court of Oyer and Terminer was fast approaching.

CHAPTER TEN

SEPTEMBER 19ᵀᴴ, 1692

"Would Martha Dutch please take the stand?" Hathorne asked, prompting a young woman in her twenties forward. She quickly vowed her oath, one hand on the Bible, and judging by her nervous glance at the holy tome, she feared the repercussions of the lies about to leave her mouth.

The last time Alice stood in this courtroom, Bridget Bishop and Sarah Good and many others had still been alive. That had been in May. But today dated September ninth. Alice had spent her summer in the dungeons, escaping at night to fight the demons who sought to ruin this town.

"Your deposition, Miss Dutch."

Clearing her throat nervously, she glanced at Alice before fearfully adverting her eyes. Unlike the others, Martha feared Alice, but not because of witchcraft. Martha was about to falsely accuse her, providing false evidence that would be used to justify her execution. In her soul, Martha knew it to be wrong, enough to be fearful of how God would punish her, but she committed the fraud, anyway.

"Not two years past, John Jarman and his crew were coming in from sea. I stood with Goody, waiting for our husbands to return from their latest voyage. As we watched the sails grow larger, the ship coming closer to port, I said to her, 'What a great mercy it is to see them come home, and through mercy, my husband had gone and come home many times. I pray he will walk off that ship, that he will return from this voyage as well.' But Alice answered with a morbid prophecy, 'No, never more in this world.'"

Alice shook with silent rage, her hands curling into fists within the folds of her skirts. She had not stood on the dock with Martha Dutch, not since the day their husbands departed. She never spoke those words to Martha, hardly knowing Martha apart from their husbands both being mariners. The *lies*. Why would Alice bother with Martha when she had her own husband to worry about? And a daughter to grieve, stillborn to the knowledge of the town.

"When I asked her to elaborate, she refused. I vehemently accused her of speaking ill of my husband and me. I prodded her for why she suggested such a grave, hateful thought, but then her words came to pass. The ship docked, and we watched, waiting for both our husbands to walk onto the pier, but when the last man left, neither of our husbands had returned. I rushed to the ship, climbing aboard, searching frantically for my husband, but he was nowhere to be found. Alice did no such thing to search for her husband. She stood solemnly, unmoving, as the ship captain approached her. Rushing back, I made it in time to hear him tell her the news.

"My husband died abroad. There was no mistake. Her prophecy came to pass, no doubt because she knew he was dead. For she colluded with the Devil during a Blood Sacrament, the most unholy of ceremonies, to rid this world of my husband." Martha gripped the arms of her chair until her knuckles whitened, her body shaking with fury. "She serves the Devil, working to kill the righteous and holy, and through her witchcraft, she killed my husband," Martha Dutch screamed the accusation, hurtling her words toward Alice, venom in her eyes, and it all made sense.

"Liar!" Alice screamed, losing her temper for the first time throughout her trial. "You are nothing more than a scheming liar, an attention seeking, desperate wench, Martha Dutch. Or do you forget? I lost my husband the same day?" Alice choked on a sob. "You think I wanted him to die? That I wanted to lose my closest companion, the man who was by my side every day of our lives?" She slammed her fist on the railing of the penalty box. "Enough already," she screamed, hot tears pricking her dark green eyes. "Enough. Either convict me, or do not, but do not sit here and accuse me of killing your husband when the Ocean took my husband the same as She stole yours."

Hathorne eased back against his chair, a triumphant smirk on his face. He had won, and he knew it. Alice had taken everything he had thrown her way, and not once did she break, but when Martha brought Alice's deceased husband into this battle, she lost all semblance of self-control. She cracked. And it would be the death of her.

Alice had known her husband would die, as she had seen the ship wrecked at the bottom of the ocean, along with all those on board. Martha was not accusing Alice of witchcraft for the same reasons as the others—she accused Alice because Martha blamed her for her husband's death. It was not rational, but for Martha, it was easy to blame the woman who gave her the bad news on the wharf the day the men departed, to blame the messenger rather than the world. She sought closure by bringing Alice to justice.

The fury in Alice's gaze made Martha crumble in on herself, trying to make herself as small as possible, as if she could hide from Alice's ire. Grief was set aside as unadulterated hatred poured out of Alice, all of it directed at Hathorne and Martha. If looks could kill, they would both be dead a thousand times over. Alice *could* kill them with a look, but it would prove her to be the witch they accused her of.

Ignoring her outburst, Hathorne banged his gavel, and called another witness to the stand to give another outrageous deposition against Alice. He called Sarah Bibber, May Walcott, Abigail Hobbs, Elizabeth Hubbard, and Ann Putnam to the stand. Each of them spoke filthy lies against Alice, accusing her of not just witchcraft. Because she was guilty of that, but she was not guilty of serving the Devil as the deluded girls claimed.

Countless men, women, and children played a hand during these trials, and had a single one of them acted any different, Alice... well, Alice would likely still be standing in the penalty box because Hathorne wanted it so, but the others, the innocents, would not be doomed to their fates.

The witnesses were mostly young women, the oldest of whom was a few years Alice's senior, but the Court and people of Salem Township believed them despite the lack of consistency across the stories. The only commonality between their tales was their accusations of Alice colluding with the Devil, which grants her powers to spin her witchcraft. Nothing else was remotely similar.

One girl accused her of killing animals and livestock, another said she was responsible for killing several of the townsfolk, and another accused her of sending animals to attack the town. Even Hathorne's face conveyed skepticism. Not that he would admit it since he knew they were lying, but if he could not pretend like these depositions were legitimate, how did anyone believe this blatant show?

But Alice knew it did not matter. So many had perished or been accused during the Trials that people were too afraid to come to her defense for fear of being the next to be accused.

Hathorne excused Ann Putnam from the stand and called Mary Warren forward to testify a second time, probably because, as the oldest, she was the most convincing actress of them all.

Mary did so eagerly, practically bouncing to the stand. She repeated her deposition from May, but this time, she added a few more embellishments, going so far as to accuse Alice of killing several men during the Blood Sacrament. She claimed she witnessed Alice sacrificing humans and animals, as well as possessing animals to attack the town, and that Alice had drowned a boy in the Salem Harbor after killing a man at sea. Alice had to admit, Mary excelled at weaving together the other girls' testimonies, closing the gaps in the stories, giving more credibility to the others.

After Mary Warren finished giving her testimony for a second time, she stepped down from the stand to retake her seat in the pew alongside the other witnesses. The Court officials, including Hathorne and Corwin, left the hall, exiting the chamber through a side door to a simple conference room. Only the men serving on the Court entered, leaving Alice, the trial attendees, and jailers in the courtroom.

When the door slammed shut behind the Court, the room filled with the hushed chatter of the observers, discussing the depositions and whether they believed Alice to be guilty, or if the stories were nothing more than hearsay. The only people not discussing the trial were the townsfolk who were actually witches, who knew this was a sham and that Alice was the last person on earth to serve the Devil. For what Salem Witch, chosen by Heaven, colluded with evil?

Alice's back faced the crowd, and for the first time during her trial, her shoulders hunched as she rounded in on herself, releasing an exasperated sigh. Her eyelids fluttered closed, and she took three deep, calming breaths to steady her shaking body. When her eyes flew open, steely resolve swam in their depths, but also a profound sense of knowing. Alice knew with absolute certainty what fate awaited her.

Thirty minutes passed before the Court returned to the courtroom to pass judgement on Alice. As the Court found their seats overlooking the hall, the attendees continued to whisper, discussing what a bad omen it was to have the Court reach a decision so quickly.

When the last judge took his seat, Hathorne stood and banged his gavel three times, quieting the room into an uneasy silence, waiting with bated breath for Alice's verdict.

Hathorne cleared his throat before addressing the room. "Alice Parker, also known as Goody Parker, on the charges of witchcraft, murder, and collusion with the Devil, the Court of Oyer and Terminer hereby finds you... guilty on all accounts. At this time, you will return to the dungeons to await your sentence. At anytime, if you desire, you may admit to your crimes and repent your sins. If you provide the Court the names of your co-conspirators, the Court will take this into account during your sentence."

The crowd gasped in horror, mostly the other witches and humans who were against the witch trials.

Alice did not flinch as the bailiff clamped manacles around Alice's wrists, binding her hands behind her, as if the shackles could prevent her from using magic.

Several townsfolk leapt to their feet, shouting at the Court and the jailer hauling Alice away. Fire flashed in Alice's eyes, and unexpectedly, she turned to the crowd and whistled, abruptly silencing the hall as every eye turned to her.

"I am innocent," Alice growled. "I see no evil, speak no evil, and hear no evil. I have never served the Devil, nor will I ever. I maintain my innocence, from now until my dying breath. As a show of good faith and to demonstrate I have nothing to hide, I shall go to the dungeons willingly. May you take that into account during my sentencing."

With that, Alice turned on her heel, yanking her chains from the jailer's hands, and marched out of the courthouse. For Alice cared not about her sentence, but that these blasted trials came to a quick end. Not waiting for the jailer, Alice strode down the street, hurriedly striding past the houses and stores lining the road until she came to an intersection. Turning North, she headed up the road for the building with an attached sign that read, "Salem Penitentiary."

The jailer was scrambling to catch up when Alice stopped in front of the prison, waiting patiently for the puffing jailer, to unlock the door. Not bothering to wait for the jailer, Alice charged through the door and stomped down the hallway, determined to take her fate into her own hands in whatever way she could. She would not allow the jailer to lead her to her prison. If she must endure hell, she would walk through it like she owned the place.

The jailer lumbered after her, panting from his futile attempt to catch her. Lucky for him, she did exactly as she said and walked into her prison cell when he unlocked the door. The jailer threw the iron bar door closed, causing the cage to rattle. He muttered something under his breath about crazy witches then, stomped away, giving

Alice privacy as she embraced her mother, Martha, with whom she shared a cell, along with her father.

Pulling back, Martha placed a hand gingerly against Alice's cheek.

"Well? What was their verdict, Alice?" Giles asked. The jailers placed the family in a cell together, a small mercy, probably because of the overflow in the cells caused by the number of witch arrests.

Alice released a heavy sigh. "No better than anyone else's. Unsurprisingly, they found me guilty on all accounts of witchcraft and conspiring with the Devil."

"Oh, for Heaven's sake," Martha snapped. "Based on what evidence?"

"Only testimonies given by Westgate and the six little girls who inflicted this plight on our town to begin with. Though plenty of townsfolk, whom I have never met, have stories of how they have witnessed my witchcraft."

"If only they knew—" Giles began.

"They cannot," Alice cut him off with a flourish of her hand. "For one, humans would never believe such a thing, and as it stands, several of their kind have spoken against my verdict, and more are working to put an end to the trials altogether."

Martha remained silent, a pensive expression on her face as she studied her daughter. "Alice, honey, you are too important to the world to be stuck in this cell, unable to... to prepare for your last Trial. You can escape, leave this place, and go somewhere you will be safe."

"No." Alice shook her head adamantly. "Absolutely not. If I escaped, they would not only blame you, but it would be the ammunition they need to fully condemn me as a witch."

Martha opened her mouth to argue, but Alice continued before she could speak a word.

"But more importantly, little more than two weeks remains until I turn seventeen. It is my responsibility to stay and protect the people. I can survive two more weeks in this hole if it means I will share my people's fate."

"Alice, how do you possibly expect to master Spirit while stuck in this cage?" her father challenged. "You should go. We will survive."

Alice went silent for a long time, staring past the bars of her cage to survey the two women imprisoned in the cell across from her. Finally, she said, "Hathorne is a demon."

Martha inhaled sharply, and her eyes widened in horror. Giles ran a hand over his balding head as a curse left his lips. Alice had not shared this knowledge before, hoping she could protect them from the evil she now faced, but she had failed in that, so her parents deserved to know what they faced.

"Not a regular demon, either. He's stronger than the rest, more powerful. More evil. He is one of the Seven."

"No," Martha gasped, her face paling at Alice's answer. Giles's body went rigid with fear, paralyzed by the mere mention of the Seven.

"So, you see, I must stay. This is to be my final Trial. This is the Salem War—the sins of men and demons against the virtues of humankind and the blessings of the Creator." Alice turned to look her mother dead in the eye, fire glinting in her hunter green eyes. "And I intend to win."

Martha and Giles lay on the ground, curled up in one another's arms, shivering from the cold, while Alice paced the cramped cell. A week had passed since she was convicted as a witch, but she had not heard a peep from Hathorne and his court. The silence was more disconcerting than anything else.

As she walked, she cast concerned glances at her parents, worry twisting her lips into a frown. Her magic unfurled around her, invisible to the naked eye. Warmth infused the cell as Alice's fire magic warmed the air and the elderly couple. Their shaking bodies slowly stilled, and they relaxed into each other's arms, their sleep undisturbed.

Hathorne appeared on the other side of the cell bars, as though he materialized from thin air, startling Alice enough that she let out a gasp.

"You," she growled loud enough to startle her parents awake.

Hathorne smiled cruelly at her. "Yes, me." He beckoned to someone out of sight of the cell. Corwin and Noyes stepped forward, along with two burly jailers. One jailer stepped forward to unlock the cell, wrenching the cell door open. None of the cell occupants moved an inch.

"What do you want?" Alice snarled at the demon.

"Nothing from you," Corwin sauntered into the cell, only to receive a stinging slap across the face from Alice. He stumbled back, holding his red cheek with his hand.

"Why you little—" Corwin made to lunge at her, but Hathorne restrained him, gesturing to the large jailers to get on with it.

The jailer who unlocked the cell hurried forward to grab Alice by the throat. Lifting her into the air, he spun and slammed her into the brick wall. The wind whooshed from her lungs as she hit the wall, followed by a sickening crack as her head smacked the stone. Martha cried out for her daughter from where she huddled in the corner, Giles's arms wrapped tightly around her.

Despite the blood dripping from the back of her skull, Alice clung to consciousness, even with the vice-like grip cutting off her air supply. Alice's hands yanked on the jailer's wrists, desperately trying loosen his grip so she could suck in oxygen. She kicked her legs frantically, aiming between his legs. But his reach was too far, even for her long legs, so she could not land a blow.

While the jailer restrained Alice, his colleague squeezed into the cell, reaching for Martha. She screamed, scrabbling into her husband's arms, but when the jailer's hand clamped around her forearm, the Coreys were useless against the force he used to rip her away from her husband. The jailer threw Martha against the wall, smacking her head against the stone. He lunged at Giles, grabbing the elderly man by the few strands of his wispy hair, long from months spent in a cell.

Alice's eyes went wide with shock, and she fought frantically against the man suffocating her. Martha was in a daze from hitting her head. As she pushed to her hands and knees, she vomited bile onto the dirt floor before collapsing.

The jailer wrenched Giles free of the cell, and Hathorne secured manacles around his wrists and ankles. The other jailer dropped Alice to flee the cell.

Alice dropped to the floor in a heap, sucking in a life-giving breath before lunging at the bars. Her hands hit the cell door with such force, the metal hinges whined.

"Father," she screamed as the men hauled Giles down the dank corridor. But it was useless. The men disappeared from sight, except Hathorne, who stood outside her cell, looking upon her in perverted delight.

"You will pay for this." She spat at him.

His smile twisted into a devilish grin. "Really? Because from where I am standing, it appears I have already gotten away with it."

Raw magical power soared out of Alice and smacked into Hathorne, throwing him against the metal bars of the opposite cell. He crashed into the dirt floor, but rose to his feet in an instant, staring at Alice with rage, and possibly a hint of fear.

"Oh, now that will not do. I will take care of you next," he threatened before sauntering merrily down the corridor, Alice glaring daggers at his back until he disappeared from sight.

Alice sat on the dirt floor of the dungeon, her legs crossed, spine erect, and eyes closed.

As a true earth witch, Alice stayed grounded to this plane, but as the Salem Witch with the power of Spirit at her disposal, Alice was not limited by the same magical constraints as her fellow earth elementals.

She could astral project. She had done it to see Sarah Good's execution, but now... now it was her father's death she sought, and perhaps the part of her that could not bear to watch his soul part from this earth grounded her to her earthly body. Emotion clogged her throat, and Alice forced it away, meditating instead on her spirit so it might detach from its earthly vessel, at least temporarily.

"Alice, are you there? Can you see him?" Martha asked for the tenth time.

Air magic wrapped around their cell, silencing their words from drifting to the other prisoners, many of whom were ignorant humans, unaware of who dwelled in their midst.

"Ugh," Alice groaned. "No, mother. I am not astral projecting yet, and I will not detach from my physical body if you keep asking. I need quiet. I have only attempted this magic once before."

Closing her eyes, Alice burrowed into her stomach, where a pool of green and gold power swirled with magic. Seizing hold of her magic, she reached for Spirit, for the golden lightning that came so easily to her.

Brace yourself, daughter. When all seems lost, remember a thread of hope is a powerful thing. Do not let evil extinguish your faith.

A shock of lightning coursed through Alice at her mother's words, ripping her soul from her body and spiriting her spectral form through space so she stood in the courtroom.

Glaring at the Court of Oyer and Terminer overseeing the room with their dark auras, Alice's eyes cut into the cowards. Her specter shook with rage as her hands curled into fists.

Hathorne's eyes sliced into her, flashing a dark blue.

Alice gasped, stumbling backward until her spirit body passed through the penalty box. Hathorne could see her standing there in her astral form. And those blue eyes... not like normal human blue, but a blue from the darkest depths of Hell. The flash of color of his eyes at her trial was enough to prove to Alice that he was who she suspected. He was Lust Incarnate.

Inside the penalty box, Alice stood beside her adoptive father. Giles, at eighty years old, stood with a fierce defiance that Alice herself had embodied over the years. He was not her biological father, but she wondered... perhaps she inherited the trait from him simply by being raised as his daughter.

Those ridiculous girls—more like serpents if you asked Alice—stood off to the side, waiting to be called on by Hathorne like the loyal dogs they were. Alice did not know if Hathorne possessed the ability to pry into the girls' minds and manipulate them, or if the girls themselves were evil little beasts, devoid of humanity, but Alice's fingers twitched with the desire to wrap around their throats and shake them until their pathetic whines died with them.

But she could not do that as a specter. Not that she would if she were physically present, but the urge remained.

Alice was thankful that she sent Ariel away with Elizabeth and convinced the townspeople her child was stillborn. It was not hard to accomplish with her mourning being genuine.

"I will not submit myself to trial by a jury who has already determined my guilt." Giles pounded a fist against the wooden banister of the penalty box.

Intuition slammed into her like a wave. Giles knew as well as her—he would not escape this trial alive, but he had older children, biological children his first two wives bore him long before Alice came along. If the Court convicted him as a witch, Alice's adoptive siblings would not receive their inheritance. And no doubt the Putnams would claim it instead.

He was right, of course. The same vile children who condemn the other men and women to death stood in the courtroom, accusing Giles of witchcraft. A conviction would be inevitable if he stood trial. But what was the alternative?

No, Giles would not yield. Alice could see the steely mettle in his eyes. He would not admit to being a witch and his refusal to stand trial was to avoid conviction. Instead, he would undergo a torturous death, so his children would inherit his wealth instead of Putnam.

Perhaps her father had not been the kindest man, nor the most considerate of others, but he was fiercely loyal to his kin. He did not deserve this any more than the other mortals accused. None had colluded with the Devil—the irony was that Hathorne was in league with the Devil.

"No man nor woman who pleaded not guilty before this assembly of fools, who believe the absurd stories of pompous little girls, has been cleared. I will not trust my fate to you. I will take what death you put me to rather than be found guilty of this ridiculous accusation of witchcraft."

Hathorne sighed, shaking his head like he was disappointed in the outcome, but the evil glint of hellish blue light in his eyes said otherwise. "Then it is with deep sorrow that I sentence you to *peine forte et dure*." There was a collective gasp of appall from the room. "Death by crushing."

Alice nearly fainted.

No. Not this.

Peine forte et dure was outlawed by the Plymouth Colony government, for it violated the Puritan provisions of the Body of Liberties.

Surely, they could not condemn him to such a death.

But as she glared into those evil eyes, at the sadistic smirk twisted Hathorne's face, and Alice realized he was gloating. He wanted someone like Giles to stand mute against the court so he could dole out this punishment. He was truly evil incarnate. And Alice had to stop him.

Alice once again projected herself from her body, sending her spirit to the dreaded gallows. But unlike with Sarah Good's execution, Alice harbored a splitting headache from lying awake all night, crying with Martha. The Court had not permitted Giles to say goodbye, keeping the family separated. It was cruel in the truest sense of the word.

Unable to watch as Giles was forced to his back and a boulder was lowered on top of him, Alice trained her gaze on Hathorne, knowing he could sense her magical presence.

The Salem Witch, master of four elements, could fend off a Prince of Hell, but she was useless to save her father's life. She had considered it, of course, offering Giles and Martha an escape, but they refused to leave without her. Giles said he was too old to run, and it would only give cause to Hathorne to convict him and seize the lands that, by law, belonged to Giles's children.

If only she could master Spirit.

But today was September nineteenth, and her birthday on September twenty-third was mere days away, and her Trial had not been triggered. And from a dungeon cell, Alice had little hope of Gabriel descending to Earth to initiate it.

All this power, and she was useless as the judges placed another stone atop her adoptive father.

"Confess!" Hathorne shrieked, his demands echoed by Sherriff Corwin and Reverend Corwin, the wicked brothers.

Giles merely shook his head as he turned red in the face from the literal pressure bearing down on him.

"Another," Hathorne growled at the sheriff, who gleefully obliged.

Giles grunted under the added weight, but he refused to speak and confess his guilt.

"Confess," Hathorne shouted, a deranged look of sadistic glee and frustration mixing on his face. Frustration that Giles refused to bend to his will, but glee at the torture of a human soul.

And on it went for what seemed like hours. Hathorne yelling at Giles to confess, only to receive silent defiance from the stubborn old man, until the weight pressing on Giles was too much.

It was obvious to Alice, to the others gathered at the gallows, and to Hathorne, that Giles had only minutes until he departed from this world.

"Any last words, Giles Corey?" Hathorne sneered at Giles from where he loomed, casting a shadow over Giles's slowly yielding body.

"More weight," Giles uttered.

Alice swallowed roughly, wrapping a hand around her throat as tears streamed from her eyes. There was no greater terror than watching someone you love fall before you. At least Alice could spare Martha that pain.

Another stone dropped on Giles's chest. Alice squeezed her eyes shut, refusing to watch, but that did not protect her from the gruesome noise as Giles breathed his last breath.

Forcing down the bile searing her throat, Alice opened her eyes to find Hathorne, covered in a splatter of blood, angrily wiping at his clothes as Sheriff George Corwin beat Giles's corpse with a cane out of rage.

The only father Alice had ever known was dead.

Giles deprived Corwin and the Putnams of stealing yet another victim's estate, and Alice's brother, John, would inherit the land. She prayed her adoptive siblings, who left Salem before Giles married Martha and adopted Alice, would be spared from this insanity.

No. She did not pray. *She* was the Salem Witch. She would spare them from the pain Giles suffered, even if it meant suffering herself.

Suffering was a feeling she had grown accustomed to these last seven years, for the Trials had not been kind to her, and she finally realized why. If it were not for the Trials forging her into a superior witch, she would crumble before the Darkness she now faced.

Her eyes fluttered shut, her eyelids suddenly heavy, and her spirit rushed to the dungeons, slamming into her body so forcefully, she sucked in a gasping breath.

"What? What did you see, Alice?" Martha frantically asked.

But Alice could not meet her eye, instead averting her gaze as she said, "Giles is dead. And we are certain to be next."

Two jailers opened a cell at the opposite end of the corridor. One jailer entered with manacles, only to exit with two men chained around the wrists. The jailer escorted the men from the jail, then returned with more manacles. They opened another cell to shackle three older women and led them outside.

"What is going on out there?" Alice muttered from where she stood pressed against the cell bars, trying to see around the corner to the end of the hall.

Nausea slammed into Alice's stomach like a punch to the gut, and her intuition told her nothing good was to come of the commotion outside her cell.

For today was September twenty-second, the day before her seventeenth birthday, and her Trial of Spirit had not yet begun. But she was not dead either, a miracle from Heaven that she did not understand, but a blessing she knew would not last.

"Alice, step away from the bars. Do not attract attention."

Alice frowned but did as Martha bid her.

The jailers pulled another woman from a cell, then returned with three sets of manacles. As the jailers appeared before Alice and Martha, Alice instinctively stepped in front of her mother, sheltering Martha with her body.

"What is going on?" Alice demanded.

The jailers ignored her as they unlocked the door.

"Sir," she tried again. "I implore you to inform us of what you intend to do. Do we not have a right to know our fates?"

"Is it not obvious?" answered a cold, vindictive voice belonging to neither jailer. Hathorne emerged from the shadows. If Alice had not already suspected, Hathorne's ability to appear at will confirmed he was a demon Prince, for only a Prince could wield such considerable power. "Today you will pay for your crimes."

Martha's face blanched sheet white, and she buried her face in Alice's shoulder, tears streaking down her cheeks as she struggled to maintain her composure. Alice wrapped an arm around her, pulling Martha's body into her own, as though she could save her mother from Hathorne's "justice".

"Excuse me," Alice's voice dripped with sarcasm before switching to disdain. "I was under the impression I was not going to be executed today. On what grounds did you decide to sentence us?"

"You are a witch," Hathorne hissed at her. "And all witches must die."

While Alice's attention was on Hathorne, the jailer rushed forward and grabbed Martha by her bonnet, wrenching her from Alice's arms. Alice reached for her, only for the other jailer to clamp a set of manacles on her wrists, binding them. Hathorne gleefully bound Martha's hands with another set and held her by the chains. The two jailers cornered Alice, using the walls of the cell to their advantage. Even with her hands bound, the jailers could sense the threat Alice posed.

But she was a witch, not a soldier trained in physical combat. All these years, she learned magic, not fighting.

The jailer on her right lunged forward. Alice swung her hands up, attempting to use the manacles as a weapon to hit the jailer, but opened herself, allowing the jailer to grab the chains linking her hands. He thrust up, forcing her hands above her head. The other jailer lunged, forcing the second set of manacles around Alice's ankles.

And what did it matter? Even if Alice incapacitated the jailers, Hathorne held Martha, and only magic could save them both, and in doing so, they would condemn themselves and give validity to Hathorne's claims so he could continue the witch trials. No. The Earth was patient. It waited and listened for its opportunity to strike. And so would Alice.

Once she was bound, the two jailers lifted her, one holding the chains around her wrists and the other holding her by the chains around her ankles. Hathorne led the way, pulling Martha roughly by the arm. Despite being practically dragged by Hathorne, Martha snuck glances over her shoulder, her features laced with worry for her daughter.

The party paraded out of the prison into the gray, overcast day. The weather was as dreary and depressing as the events soon to transpire, as though Mother Earth herself wept for the lives to be lost this day.

Hathorne flung Martha to the ground, sending her rolling through the dirt until she collided with the side of a wooden cart that held the other accused witches. Alice bucked from where she was suspended between the two jailers, struggling to free herself so she could run to her mother's aid.

When Hathorne yanked Martha up by her hair and flung her into the cart with the others, whose hands were bound with rope. No doubt Hathorne's unnecessary roughness was for no reason other than to antagonize Alice.

The jailers tossed Alice into the cart that would bring her and the other victims to their deaths. Martha Corey, Mary Eastey, Wilmot Redd, Samuel Wardwell Sr., Ann Pudeator, Margaret Scott, Mary Parker, and of course, Alice Parker.

Who would be the last so-called "witches" to die in these trials? When would the slaughter end?

Alice's entire body twitched, and her magic sang through her veins, eager to jump into the fray, ready to wipe away the vermin littering the earth. She wanted nothing more than to attack the jailers and free the wrongfully accused witches.

Even if she could change what happened, would it do any good? Or would the Trials gain traction? If she had mastered Spirit, would this be happening?

Everything happens in its own time, according to the plans of the Universe. The Creator is never too early, nor too late, but right on time. Uriel's melodious voice drifted through Alice's head, and she closed her eyes, treasuring the sound as she was carted to her death.

Alice did not fear death. No. She would meet her mother there. And her husband was on the other side. That was not why she did not wish to die. She had survived too much to leave this earth without defeating Hathorne and ending the Salem War.

A jailer slapped the donkey on its hindquarters, but it did not budge. It did not even flinch, but stood there, chewing on the straw of hay sticking out of his mouth.

The jailers glanced uncertainly at one another as the crowd of townsfolk looked on with curiosity. He hit the donkey again, but the animal made no indication that he felt the stinging slap. The second jailer tried his hand at it, smacking the donkey's bottom so hard, the sound echoed, yet the donkey remained unmoved.

"Ah, bugger this." The first man spat. "We are gonn' have to pull the dang thing ourselves."

The second jailer reluctantly followed suit to detach the donkey from the cart. Between the two men, they made quick work of it, but when it came time to move the cart, the two men alone could not pull eight people. The younger jailer slipped and face planted in the mud. Not two minutes prior, the donkey had stood right where his face landed, and Alice swallowed a snort at his misfortune.

Cursing, the man covered in donkey poop went to gather men from the Court to help move the cart. Half an hour later, he returned with eight other men to push the cart and they set to it. But even with ten men pushing, the cart resisted them. Like the Universe did not want the accused men and women to be executed. It was slow, grueling work for the men, but Alice could not muster an ounce of sympathy. In fact, she found a certain satisfaction when one of the wheels became stuck in a crevice in the road to Gallows Hill. Alice wondered which idiot decided the gallows should be located so far from the jail?

A man departed from the others, running along the path to the gallows, no doubt to fetch Hathorne and the Corwins, but it was not just the vile men whom the man returned with. The "witnesses", the brutal children who caused so much suffering with their despicable actions, approached the cart, the Putnam brat leading the bunch.

Ann Putnam Junior stepped closer to the cart full of condemned witches, then threw herself back, shaking her body ridiculously. Corwin and the cart man each grabbed the girl by a hand and hauled her away from the cart until she stopped shaking. But the other girls followed suit, each stepping bravely toward the cart, then acting absurdly, as though an unseen, spectral force attacked them, until they were pulled away from the cart.

"They are using the Devil's dark magic to stall the cart," Ann accused. "You must hurry and free it from their grasp."

With renewed vigor inspired by fear, the cart men attacked the cart wheels with a strength they previously lacked, but Alice felt no inclination to make it easy. Willing the earth to soften, she let the wheel sink farther into the mud.

"Their magic—the Devil, he is—"

A harsh wind blew from the east, slamming into the foolish children and pushing them to the ground like they were chaff in the wind.

Struggling to her feet against the magical squall, Ann shot a daggered glare at Alice. As a witch, she surely sensed Alice's powers were the source of the unnaturally forceful wind. "They can assault us from afar," Ann cried, pointing an accusing finger at Alice. "They cannot be suffered to live any longer, or we will all be doomed."

"Now, now, Ann." Hathorne patted Ann's shoulder with a meaty hand. "As a righteous man of the Lord, I shall free the cart from their tainted magic."

Moving to the back of the cart, Hathorne's gaze met Alice's hunter green eyes. Indigo light flashed through his eyes as he lifted the cart with ease, then pushed it forward, freeing it from its trap.

Moving forward unhindered, the cart hauled Alice and the others to their deaths.

CHAPTER ELEVEN

SEPTEMBER 22ND, 1692

One by one, each of the accused was released from the cart to be pulled up the wooden stairs of the platform and placed at the noose. Some struggled against their captors, others wailed, some cried, and others went quietly, resigned to their fate.

But Alice would not go without a fight, or at least without making a scene, kicking and screaming the whole while. She bit at her captor, wriggling her shackle-bound hands, futilely trying to free herself. Invisible magic flew from her hands, undetectable by the humans present. The manacles binding her hands and ankles came loose, and she wrenched her arms free.

Spinning on her heel, she smashed her palm into her jailer's nose, forcing him to release her to grab his face as a torrent of blood flowed from it. Four more jailers rushed to contain her, each grabbing an appendage, then hauled her up to the platform of the gallows like a sack of potatoes, held by her arms and legs.

They dropped her on the platform, eliciting a heavy thump as her body smacked against the planks. Alice shot to her feet, but as she rose, Hathorne appeared before her faster than the human eye could track. He slipped a noose of rope around her neck, pulling it tight so it pressed on her airway.

Alice lashed out, punching at the demon, but Corwin appeared behind her and wrapped his arms around her torso, pinning her arms to her side so she could not fight back. Another man re-secured metal shackles on her wrists and ankles. Once she was subdued, Corwin released her, so she stood on the door that would drop out from under her feet to herald her toward the afterlife.

Alice turned, her eyes searching for Martha, who was cruelly placed at the opposite end to separate mother and daughter. Martha's gaze locked with Alice's and with tears welling in her eyes, she mouthed, "I love you."

With wet cheeks, Alice nodded despite the noose choking her. She mouthed back to her mother, "I love you, too."

"Last chance," Hathorne cackled.

Alice whipped her head around, her gaze snapping to Hathorne as he stared her down, not bothering to glance at the other victims.

"Admit to your crimes and repent before the Lord. Do so now or die knowing you forsake the Lord. Do so to save your immortal soul, for this life has ended for you either way."

Hathorne approached the victims one by one, starting with Martha. "Repent," he spat at her. When she refused, he struck her with his open palm, and fury burned within Alice.

Moving to Mary Eastey, he demanded she repent. But she also refused, enduring a physical blow from Hathorne instead. Down the line he went, receiving silence or a definitive no from each victim. None of them gave him the sick satisfaction by admitting to crimes they did not commit.

Never in her life did Alice experience such raw hatred burning in her veins.

"What say you, *Goody*?" He smiled wickedly, proud of himself for his mocking use of her nickname. "Do you repent your sins?"

Spittle smacked Hathorne in the eye. Wiping Alice's spit from his face, Hathorne's eye flashed indigo as he struck her.

Alice's earth magic, the magic that loved her most, rushed over her skin, turning her cheek to steel in place of flesh. Hathorne's hand struck her metal cheek, and Hathorne's hand shattered with a sickening crunch. Alice's lips twisted with smug satisfaction at the shock and pain on Hathorne's face, right before she head butted him in the nose.

He staggered back, holding his bloody nose with his unbroken hand. "Repent, demon," he shouted, flourishing his broken hand at her. "Or die with your sins and descend into Hell."

With fierce determination, Alice growled, "Bury me shallow. I will be back."

She punctuated her warning with a menacing glare at her prosecutors. Several of the townsfolk flinched, as though she were a serpent striking with her fangs, but Hathorne's only reaction was an evil grin as he motioned for the executioner to pull the lever.

Alice almost missed the flash of indigo in his eyes. Almost.

A gasp escaped her lips as the door dropped under her. There was a brutally sharp snap in her neck, and Alice's body went lax as she slowly twirled in a circle.

Alice felt every bit of what happened to her as white light surrounded her. As a Nephilim, her soul had not yet severed from her body, not until she entered the Garden. But Alice ignored Amara, the personification of Death and the first Salem Witch, as she materialized beside Alice with her candy apple red hair and jade green eyes.

"What a sad thing it is to see eight firebrands of Hell hanging there," Noyes remarked, shaking his head sadly.

Hathorne stood on the platform of the gallows, preaching to the town and looking mighty pleased with himself as a man untied Alice's noose, and her body crumpled in the dirt. Her corpse was carried away and tossed on top of the pile of dead like she was a bale of hay to be carted off.

Anger flooded Alice's soul as she yearned to set fire to Hathorne's soul. Not that he had one.

"It is a special kind of torture," Amara stated solemnly. "To feel everything that is happening to you, but be paralyzed, unable to do anything with your own body."

Alice stood with one foot in the earthly plane and one in the spiritual realm. She could see Earth in her mind's eye, though her soul saw the bright light of Heaven around her and the golden gates beyond the clouds.

"You can sense Earth because of your mother's connection to the realm. No other Nephilim experiences death the way you do."

Alice did not speak as she watched in her mind as the last body was piled on the back of the cart, and the driver whipped the reins, spurring the donkey forward.

Amara did not speak, but merely took Alice by the arm and guided her to the Gates. But they walked slowly, as though Amara knew Alice needed to see what happened to her mother and father. To see what happened to her.

The journey to the field riddled with unmarked graves was not long, and the driver and his assistant made quick work of unloading the bodies and tossing them unceremoniously in shallow graves. Hurriedly, they spilled the unearthed dirt into the graves to cover the bodies, glancing nervously at the horizon as though they did not want to remain with the dead after dark.

Each body was barely covered by dirt, except for one. Alice felt every pound of dirt weighing on her, suffocating her body, pressing on her bones and organs.

No doubt Hathorne had ordered them to bury Alice deeper than the rest to spite her even in death.

The driver and his assistant finished their jobs in a rush, glancing nervously at the freshly buried, as though the dead would rise again and come for them. The men left in a hurry, spurring the donkey into a rapid trot to carry them away quickly.

With a sigh, Alice tuned out the vision of life on Earth and focused on Death.

"Hello, Amara. I remember you."

Amara smiled, her teeth filed to deadly points. "We met when your soul was created, and I told you that I was the first, but sadly not the last, and you must carry on the fight I could not end. The perpetual war against Darkness."

"Yes, but while you successfully banished Lilith to Hell, I failed to rid the world of Asmodeus. I failed the Trials."

"Did you?" Amara raised an eyebrow and gestured to Alice's head.

She looked down and gasped. Her hair was not its normal fiery red, but metallic silver that shimmered as bright as a full moon. Gingerly, Alice palmed a tuft of her hair, raising it to eye-height in disbelief. Disbelief that she was in the middle of a Trial.

Raising a hand to her cheek, she asked, "Are my eyes—"

"Hunter green," said a melodic, feminine voice that did not belong to Amara.

Alice's head snapped up, and she nearly cried at the sight of her birth mother.

Uriel, the Archangel of Earth, stood in all her Glory before her daughter. "In the realm of the Creator, souls appear exactly as they should be, and as windows to the soul, your eyes will never shine a color other than hunter green."

"Mother," Alice said breathlessly, tears of joy swimming in her eyes.

"Hello, my Little Bull," Uriel said, spreading her arms wide. Uriel smiled, her perfect teeth shining like pearls, and Alice found herself enamored. She stood seven feet tall, as tall as Gabriel, despite being female. Fiery red hair flowed in soft, vibrant waves to her waist, and forest green eyes glimmered like crystals, power ebbing and flowing within their woodsy depths. Her skin held a deep tan, darker than Alice's. Golden swirls were inked on her arms and legs, but they undulated and writhed across the surface of her skin, as though the ink were alive. Because it was.

Within the design were creatures of every kind—bunnies, squirrels, deer, bears, lions, elephants, and of course, the bull—and flora twining between them in a plethora of greens and pinks and reds. Uriel's entire body flowed with the natural order of the earth, the animals inked on her so she could watch over them. Green and gold light haloed around the archangel. Alice's signature colors.

Throwing herself at Uriel, Alice wrapped her arms around the seven-foot-tall archangel and squeezed with all the strength in her spiritual body. Uriel's gentle hand patted her on the back as the other stroked her hair.

"Now, now, my Little Bull. You were never truly alone. I have always watched over you. You just were not always aware of it."

Sniffling, Alice pulled away to gaze at her mother's glowing face. Light streamed from the tattoos painting Uriel's skin, making her glow brighter than the other archangel standing beyond her.

"Gabriel?" Alice gasped, pulling out of her mother's arms completely.

"Hello, Alice," Gabriel said warmly. "And welcome to your final Trial."

"And what is the decision I am to make in this final Trial?" Alice asked, but she turned away from Gabriel to stare at her mother instead.

"Whether to return to Earth as a Resurrected Nephilim or continue on to the Garden of Eden." Amara said, sweeping at hand out behind her, gesturing to the glowing gates. "If you return, your life will be bound to the Earth for all eternity. You will never be allowed to enter the Garden of Eden."

"It is not a simple decision, Little Bull, but it is one your soul has been prepared to make. But only you can choose your future."

"Do I have time to think about my decision?"

"Yes, but you do not have long. The soul cannot remain in this in-between space or else it will become torn, split between the worlds and susceptible to the forces of Darkness corrupting it."

"Then, before I make my final decision, I have questions," Alice said, looking between her mother and Gabriel as Amara stood silently in the background.

"Ask away, Little Bull, and we shall answer."

"Who is my father?" Alice asked. It was a question that had plagued her, though she never had much time to wonder with the Salem Witch Trials consuming her waking hours.

"John Proctor," Uriel declared, her eyes alight with adoration.

Alice threw her head back and laughed, her silver hair flying behind her. "You must be joking, Mother. John Proctor was my neighbor for half my life, and Giles despised him."

Uriel smiled knowingly. "Yes, I am aware. How do you think I selected Giles to be your adoptive father? Angels are not limited to time the way mortal experience it. I am always living in the present moment, where past, present, and future overlap. When I sent you to live with Martha, I knew Giles would court her before you were revealed as the Salem Witch. While some time passed before he officially married Martha, I tasked him with the responsibility of being a father figure to you. Giles had a colorful history with the law, and considering his reputation for lacking compassion and consideration for others in his community, I knew people would assume he and Martha conceived you out of wedlock and none would dare question him taking you in. Selfish men do not adopt orphans.

"I lived with John Proctor while pregnant with you and for another three years while we raised you. Giles was never fond of John, but he was always kind to me, though I hid my true nature from him and the other mortals in Salem, and I knew he would protect you with a certain ferocity. And his dislike of John ensured little contact between you and your father."

"But why could I not stay with my father when you left?"

Uriel's face fell, her expression dark for an angel. "Because I faked your death."

Alice stepped back, shock stunning her into silence.

"Asmodeus—the Deadly Sin of Lust and Prince of Hell—possessed Hathorne before you were born, and my presence did not deter him from seeking retribution, for I repelled him from Heaven during the Fall of Stars—our fellow angels. A Prince of Hell does not want a Nephilim living in Salem. Even as a babe, you were powerful, so he sought to kill you to prevent you from interfering with his plans. I circumvented it, but it was no longer safe for you to live openly with John, so I tricked Asmodeus into believing he succeeded, then hid you with Martha."

"That is why you left," Alice said, understanding dawning on her. "If you had stayed on Earth, Asmodeus would have known I was still alive."

"For him to think you were well and truly dead, I returned to Heaven, for what angel stays in the mortal realms if her daughter's soul returned to the Garden?"

"Asmodeus knows I am the Salem Witch, but he does not know I am Nephilim," Alice said excitedly, glancing between Amara and Uriel. "If I return, he will not expect it, for the power of resurrection does not necessarily belong to the Salem Witch. The world will believe me to be dead, so I can use my magic. I can stop this war."

Uriel's smile turned sorrowful. "If you return, you will be a master of Spirit."

"But you will also be an immortal," Amara added. "Not even death can separate your soul from the mortal lands for too long." Then she added with a wink, "Though there is always a loophole, but you may be waiting a few hundred years, depending on how the Apokalypsis War turns out."

"I can never die," Alice stated simply, yearning for the golden gates beyond Amara and the archangels. "I do not know what to do." She dropped her face into her hands.

"Then perhaps there are certain souls who can give you guidance," Gabriel rumbled.

Alice's head snapped up as she felt the arrival of two souls from within the Garden of Eden.

"Mother. Father," she exclaimed, rushing for Giles's and Martha's glowing spirits.

She slammed into them, crying tears of joy at their reunion. Alice and her mother died at the same time, but Martha must have passed on to the Garden immediately while Alice watched her body and spoke with Amara.

Pulling away, Alice gripped Martha's hands and searched Giles's eyes. "Are you two alright? Are you in the Garden?"

"We are, Alice." Martha cupped her cheek with a hand. "All is well with our souls. Rest easy knowing we are at peace in the Garden, and do not let our deaths sway your decision."

"I... I do not know what to do," Alice admitted. "A part of me wants to return and end the Salem War. I worry about what will happen to Earth if I do not. But selfishly... selfishly, my soul yearns for the Garden, for John."

"Do not let me be the one to stop you from fulfilling your true vocation, my dearest Alice."

"John," Alice said, a sob bubbling in her throat as he appeared next to her.

Her eyes locked on his, and light burst to life around their left hands. Green light shined from her ring finger as golden light streamed from John's. Angel wings, inked in swirling greens and gold and surrounded by brown vines, danced over their skin in identical tattoos.

Soulmate glyphs.

Wordlessly, he pulled her to his chest, crushing her soul against his as if he could merge them into one. Because, in a way, they were one. They did not experience their soulmate sighting on Earth, because John died before they could both turn seventeen, and both people must be adult witches before the Creator revealed their soulmates. But they knew. In their souls, they had always known they belonged to one another, marked with the blessing of the God and Goddess.

"Oh, how I have missed you, Alice."

Alice wept, her tears disappearing in the brightness of the light of Heaven around them. "I have missed you like an uprooted tree misses the earth. You are my everything."

"Not everything, Alice." John pulled away to stare into his wife's hunter green eyes. Eyes that matched his.

"I cannot return. I thought I could, but..." Alice trailed off as she clung to her husband.

"Your soul knows what to do, Alice. Do not let my presence alter your decision."

"How can it not? You are my *soulmate*, John. I just got you back, and now you want me to leave?"

"Of course, I do not want to be apart from you. But you must return," John insisted. "The fate of the world depends on it."

"But you are here." Alice cried, her chest heaving as she sobbed. "If I return without you, we will be separated for eternity."

"That is not so," John said, wiping the tears from her cheeks. "I will reincarnate into another life to be with you."

"And then what, John? You die and leave me alone again?"

"I will die, and I will rise. Again and again, until one day I can become an immortal like you. Do not allow your desire to be with me to cloud your judgement. Do not let me be the reason thousands more perish because you do not return."

Unable to speak from the emotion clogging her throat, Alice nodded, then pressed her forehead to John's, letting his thumbs brush away the tears spilling down her cheeks.

"Then I have made my decision, my love." Alice wept, knowing the pain she would inflict on herself and her soulmate. "In this life and next, right?" she whispered.

"And in every life after that," John whispered back to her.

"Make the bastards suffer, will ya?" Giles said, slicing through the tension straining the air, causing Alice and John to snort with laughter, but Martha swatted him on the arm.

"Giles," Martha chastised. "Language. We are in the presence of our Creator."

"Are we not always in the presence of the Creator?" Alice asked.

"I am always with you, Alice," spoke an ethereally feminine voice, a voice more divine than any voice that ever fell upon Alice's ears.

"But rarely do I appear in a physical form on the mortal plane, for it is unbearable to separated from God for too long, for He and I are one and the same, and duality does not bode well for our creation, but oneness and wholeness leads them to our Light."

"Goddess," Alice breathed out the word like a prayer, then bowed her head as she clapped a fist over her heart and kneeled before a perfect being of Light.

A woman with black skin that glittered like stars twinkling in the night sky materialized before Alice. Straight hair fell past her shoulders, stopping at her waist, shining with the silvery glow of a full moon. But as Alice peered into the shining silver orbs that lacked a pupil, she truly understood why her hair and eyes turned silver during a Trial. It was to reflect the appearance of the Goddess.

"Rise, Daughter of Heaven," she spoke, her white teeth flashing against the darkness of her skin, and Alice clamored to her feet, staring at the Goddess with wide eyes.

"You are here... you are with us."

"I have always been with you, my child. And I will always be with you. Whether you stay in Heaven or return to Earth, my Spirit will be there to guide you."

Alice glanced at the shimmering gates leading to the Garden. "What decision do you want me to make?" Alice asked, knowing the answer was she should go back and fulfill the destiny the Goddess had entrusted to her soul.

"I wish for you to make your own decision, Alice, for I always give my children a choice. Other than my unconditional love, free will is the greatest gift I have bestowed upon mortals."

Alice gnawed on her lip as John wrapped his arms around her from behind. How could she give this up? Her parents, her mother, even her sire who resided in the Garden, her soulmate, and the Goddess. They were all here. She could be with all of them. Except Ariel... her daughter was still alive...

And as the Nephilim of Earth, Alice felt her ties to the land, and as if the element itself knew she was considering fleeing, the plants and animals cried to her, begging their beloved daughter not to leave. How could she turn her back on Earth? On the people who needed her? On Ariel?

"What was the point of the Trials?" Alice asked. "I did not make a difference in the world, and if I do not return, then all I endured was for naught."

"Many witches mistake the Trials as mere tests to assess your physical and magical progress through the years, but my Trials are so much more. Each element and its Trial are specifically tailored to your soul to bring you closer to the essence of my Spirit until you know it as intimately as you know your own. No two Salem Witches face the same Trials. Yours are completely unique from the Salem Witch before you, and the one who will come after you will face her own unique challenges, but for each Salem Witch, the Trials are designed to teach them the same lessons. Air is wily and flighty but weens a sharp mind. Fire is alive. It breathes and grows. Water is cool and soothing, cleansing to the soul. And earth is steady and stable, just like you. So, no, if you do not return, the Trials were not a waste. The Trials brought you closer to me, and in doing so, your soul has already made your decision."

Alice glanced at her parents, then turned to John, a pained expression claiming her face. Bringing his lips to hers, she savored their kiss, a kiss beyond what they felt on the mortal plane, for their souls were connected here without a physical body to separate them.

"I love you, John," Alice whispered, choking up. "To Eden and back."

"And I love you, Alice," John whispered, wiping away her tears as he stared into her hunter green eyes. "Whether we are on Earth or in Eden, where your soul goes, I will follow for all eternity."

Alice nodded, the emotion too much for her as she turned in John's arms to face her parents. "I love you."

"And we love you. We are so, so proud of you, Alice."

Before a fresh wave of tears could consume Alice, she faced Uriel and Gabriel.

"Will you come visit?"

Uriel smiled that angelic smile, the golden tattoos on her arms glowing brighter. "Whenever you desire, you merely have to call upon me, and I will answer."

Gabriel winked an uncanny blue and white eye at her. "And you will see me more often than you think."

A laugh bubbled out of her. "I am not so sure I want to see you again, Gabriel. Every time I do, it is because of a Trial."

Uriel's laughter matched her daughter's as the Messenger Archangel rolled his eyes. "I swear, the next Trials I descend to Earth for will not be yours. Plus, I have yet to sire any children on Earth."

Alice's brow furrowed. "Children? I thought celestials could only produce one mortal heir?"

Gabriel winked at her again. "You would not believe some of the thoughts I have heard in the minds of mortals throughout the years. Who knew humans were so clever? They may have given me an idea or two." Gabriel's eyes flickered to the Goddess. "But you are almost out of time, Little Bull. Are you ready?"

"I think so." Alice pressed a kiss to John's hand, then reluctantly stepped out of his embrace with one last pained look before turning to the Goddess. "How do I know I am making the right decision?" Alice asked her creator.

The Goddess smiled at Alice, spreading her arms to embrace Alice in the most loving hug she ever received, for she was filled with the unconditional love that could only come from the Creator.

"Your soul knows the way."

CHAPTER TWELVE

THE SALEM WAR

Dusk fell over Gallow's Hill, plunging the tainted land into night.

A sickly pale hand shot up from the mound of dirt. The ground rumbled, powerful magic emanating from the closed fist. Dirt sprayed in every direction and the earth trembled in fury. Glowing green magic pulsed around the grave, building in intensity, gathering more and more earth energy in the grave.

The earth detonated, shooting pebbles and rocks like bullets from the grave. When the dust cleared, a woman hovered above the empty grave.

Hunter green light shined from her body like a beacon. Her dark red hair was knotted and mangy but drifted on an unfelt breeze. A golden light encircled the crown of her head, like the halo of an angel, and her hunter green eyes, lined with black charcoal, were on fire with anger while the powers of Heaven flowed through her veins. Green light shined in a thin band around her ring finger on her left hand, and when the light faded, a white tattoo wrapped around the finger in a ring.

Alice Parker, haggard and dirty, her torn dress covered in dirt, stood in the glory of Heaven. Only, she was no longer mortal Alice Parker. She was Alice, the Resurrected Nephilim daughter of Uriel.

She burned like ice and froze like fire, a beautifully terrifying sight to behold. A nightmare taken flesh as her entire being pulsed with gold and green light.

Alice could have spooked, but what was the fun in that? With magic at her fingertips, she stormed to the road leading from the gravesite, past Gallows Hill and into town. Still glowing with brilliant energy, she stopped to stare down the creepy, dark lane. Tree branches swayed, casting subtle shadows in the silver moonlight.

Her lips twisted into a devilish smirk. Nothing out tonight was scarier than the witch who would dole out death on this grim and ghoulish night.

As she marched onward, not a note of hesitation delayed her steps. Alice did not look anywhere but ahead, but she was not oblivious to the creatures of the forest popping up at the edge of the woods, staring at her eagerly, some of them running along the forest to keep astride with her. She did not need to look. As the Nephilim of Earth, she sensed their presence, their presence speaking to her as clearly as a human speaking aloud.

Shockwaves rippled through the earth beneath her feet. Trees swayed in toward the road, reaching out to touch her as she passed. Her green magic glowed brighter, as though it gained power with every step she took, like the plants and animals gathered were lending their power to her as she marched up the crooked wooden steps to *his* house.

Alice rapped on the door curtly, and a light leapt into existence in one of the upper windows as a candle was lit. Shuffling sounded on the other side of the door, yet Alice waited patiently, muting her magic so he did not sense her.

Judge Hathorne opened the door.

Alice watched with wicked delight as shock slapped him across the face, and he dropped the candle. He may have known she was the Salem Witch, which is why he targeted her and her family, but he was ignorant to her heritage, to the blood of angels flowing through her veins.

With a vengeful smile, she struck.

Air magic blasted Hathorne in the chest, sending him flying backward into his house and down the hall. Alice stormed in after him, thrusting out her hands and lighting the wood-paneled hall with holy flames, yet nothing burned. Yet.

Hathorne struggled to rise from where he laid crumbled on the floor against the wall. Alice had thrown him across the entire length of his house.

"W-who are y-you?" he stuttered, genuine fear overtaking his voice despite the flash of indigo in his eyes.

Alice did not speak as she called upon her third element and shot spears of ice from her palms. Not a single spear pierced Hathorne but imbedded in the wooden floor and walls around him, forming his own personal cage. The earth raged underfoot as Alice prowled forward. Plants of many varieties burst from the floorboards, vines wrapping around his appendages and thorns sinking into his flesh.

"Hello, Asmodeus," Alice snarled. "Did no one tell you?" She cocked her head at him mockingly. "There is a new Salem Witch, and she will be the end of you."

Silver washed through Alice's hair, traveling from the roots in her skull to the tips, as the power of Spirit filled her being. The golden circlet of light resting on the crown of her head glowed brighter and wings of golden wisps of Spirit sprouted from her back. Silver was the color of the Salem Witch, but the gold and green magic was inherited from her mother.

"No," Hathorne gasped. "I-it cannot be. I-I-I k-k-killed you-you i-in your-your in-infancy."

Alice smiled a truly disturbing smile. "You almost succeeded, too. If I were anyone else, I would be dead. But when I was a child, you underestimated me." She did not deign to tell him it was her mother's powers that sensed the threat and saved her, the same way Alice saved her own daughter. Let Hathorne fear her for the power she wielded—for it was power granted by the archangels.

"W-what?" Hathorne stammered, petrified from fear. "W-w-ho are you? H-how did you s-s-survive?"

"Isn't it obvious?" Alice cackled maniacally, and Hathorne failed to suppress the shiver that wracked his body. "I am the Nephilim of Earth, daughter of Uriel."

Asmodeus paled as the blood drained from his face.

"No, I—" he protested. But it was too late.

Alice stepped toward him, placing one hand on his heart and the other to his forehead. Golden light poured from her hands where they touched his skin, growing in intensity until it was too bright for the mortal eye, but Alice did not avert her gaze as her skin sparkled and Hathorne's smoked.

"My mother repelled you from Heaven, and now, I will repel you from Earth."

The Nephilim of Earth called upon the full power of Spirit and penetrated Asmodeus's mind. Her vision raced through the centuries, his memories flowing into her faster than any mortal could track, but Alice saw it all.

Alice traveled back in time to the fifteenth century, when Asmodeus first claimed possession of this body as the foolish mortal willingly relinquished his power to the Prince of Hell. Asmodeus was bound by free will and could not force any human's hand, but Heinrich Kramer, as he was known then, was dark in his soul, lusting after the power he believed Asmodeus would grant him.

Foolish mortal. He did not realize his soul would perish in the fires of Hell when the Sin of Lust consumed. Asmodeus targeted Kramer for his demented mind and to use his power and prestige in Europe to publish that horrendous document—*the Malleus Maleficarum*. The Hammer of Witches. A treatise on how to hunt, identify, and kill witches.

The inaccuracy of the document was laughable, but that was the purpose. Asmodeus did not care to hunt legitimate witches, but to spread chaos and suspicion in the world by propagating a *lust* for power amongst men, to turn neighbor against neighbor, using their fear to concoct one of the greatest horrors that would plague human and witch history.

His memories flooded Alice's mind's eye, and she flipped through scene after scene of him using dark magic to construct new personas for the mortal vessel that existed indefinitely because of his demonic magic. But indefinite did not mean unkillable.

And Alice was supernatural.

Lust was a skilled manipulator, twisting humans, animals, and witches to serve his ends. It was evil and ingenious, and through the power of the endless personas he invented for himself, Asmodeus rendered the witch hunts possible, spreading them across the old continent faster than wildfire. Throughout the years, he positioned himself so he could perpetuate the evil flood of the land. And with every life taken in the name of his cause, Lust grew stronger.

Alice realized with a start why Asmodeus attempted to ruin the world with his twisted game. Given enough time and bloodshed in the name of Lust, Asmodeus would accumulate enough darkness in the mortal realm to manifest his immortal body on Earth.

That was why he attempted to kill her as a child, and then Ariel on the night she was born. As the descendants of an angel, Alice and Ariel were the only two witches with the purity and power to combat the Darkness threatening to swallow the world. If the forces of Darkness rooted into the hearts of enough people, corrupting their hearts, it would give Asmodeus the power he needed to escape Hell in his true form—the form of a fallen angel, which was vastly more powerful than a possessed human like Hathorne.

Well, if that was what he desired, then Alice would grant it to him. Asmodeus would be weakest, his power incomplete, right after materializing fully on Earth. And with Spirit, Alice could destroy the immortal body of the fallen angel forever, preventing his full power from being unleashed on earth.

Golden light filled the hall, streaming off Alice's body like a halo. Wings of golden Spirit extended from Alice's back like an avenging angel—no, not an angel. An avenging *Nephilim*.

Eyes burning fiercely, Alice forced Hathorne's jaw down, holding it open with the power of the elements raging around her. Spirit extended from Alice and beamed into Hathorne's face, plunging down his throat.

Hathorne thrashed uncontrollably—until Alice's elements bounded him beyond movement. Spirit burrowed deep within him, down his abdomen, and into the swirling pool of indigo power at his core.

Grabbing hold of that dark magic, Alice let her light surround it, then yanked, ripping Lust from its dwelling place in the human vessel. Her light retreated from Hathorne's throat, pulling the dark entity with it.

The Darkness wriggled, frantically struggling to escape Alice's grasp. Glaring at it, she wrenched her hands off Hathorne's body, letting the vessel drop to the floorboards.

"There you are," she growled at the entity of inky indigo shadows, refusing to release it from the golden light holding it prisoner. She snarled his name, "Asmodeus."

Yanking her hand back and cupping it around the air, Alice summoned a ball of pure, unyielding Spirit to her hand, manifesting it in a ball of golden light. Thrusting her hand forward, she shoved Spirit into the undulating mass of indigo.

Heavenly power attacked the black mass, pulling and shaping it into a dark form. Muscular, sinewy limbs extended from the blob, forming two massive legs and bulging arms. A chiseled torso appeared next as the light pulled the inky darkness into the shape of a head. Light shined around the creature of the depths, burning into Asmoedeus as he released an agonized scream as the light burned him.

But Alice did not shield her eyes from the light of Heaven bright enough to blind any other mortal. She watched as it chipped away at the shadows protecting Asmoedeus's body until the Darkness abandoned his immortal body, leaving the flesh and bone of a six-foot tall man with black wings. Wings with feathers missing from the angel slowly losing the attribute that allowed him to fly through the heavenly realms.

Asmodeus's original form.

A fallen angel stood before Alice, but she did not flinch as the Prince gazed at her with hooded eyes. His scent was intoxicating—like fresh tilled soil and freshly bloomed apple blossoms—designed to seduce her. Asmodeus may have embodied the Sin of Lust, making him the single most attractive male to step foot in the mortal realm, but he was fallen for a reason.

"Hello, Alice," the Prince of Hell said in a deep, sultry voice, reaching a flawless hand up to tuck the stray hairs behind Alice's ear.

Alice smirked at Asmodeus, completely unfazed by his sexual appeal. He was not her husband, and she felt no desire to allow him to remain in her domain. Her hand snatched his wrist before he could touch her, golden Spirit shining from her palm.

Hissing, Asmodeus made to yank his hand back, but Alice held fiercely, refusing to relinquish her grip.

"Goodbye, Asmodeus," the Salem Witch growled, her hair shimmering silver from its roots to the tips as her eyes swirled like molten pools of silver.

The full power of Heaven surged through her, haloing around her and extending to Asmodeus to immerse him in a baptism of Spirit. And Spirit was death to a Prince of Hell, who had willingly fallen from Grace.

Asmodeus reared back, trying to pull out of Alice's grasp with his perfectly sculpted body, but despite his angelic form, he was pitifully weak compared to the Salem Witch who wielded power from the Creator.

A black, swirling mass of shadows leaked from every orifice of the immortal's body, hovering in the air above the fallen angel. Golden light wrapped around the entity of Darkness, the essence of the Sin of Lust, preventing it from escaping.

Asmodeus tipped his head back, releasing a guttural roar in a voice that was neither animal nor human, wholly evil and less than this world. His eyes lit up with an ominous indigo glow as his guttural roar turned hoarse, screaming through his clenched teeth.

Spirit flashed, consuming Asmodeus's angelic body, reducing him to dust, with the echo of his last scream lingering on the air. The ashes drifting down were a dark contrast against the golden light, like the stars against the night sky, but in reverse. The fallen angel, the immortal vessel of the Sin was gone.

But the entity of the Sin, the concentrated essence of Lust, remained in this mortal realm in the form of an inky indigo mass of darkness. Alice would not allow it to escape. She would not allow it freedom to wreak havoc on her world. Green and golden light burst from Alice like the northern lights illuminating the night sky.

Inky indigo tendrils shot at Alice in a desperate attempt to kill her before she removed the Sin's taint from this land, only to be burned into oblivion by the holy display of destructive light shining from Alice's palm. Light clawed at the darkness, shredding it, consuming it, inch by inch until the tendrils were gone. Then, Alice's light, the power of Spirit, slammed into the Sin with a searing force, a force that could not be diminished, for it was the power of Heaven. Alice closed her eyes, giving herself over fully to the angels, to the Goddess, to let them use their power through her immortal vessel to banish the Sin. Brilliant light pierced through her closed eyelids, and her eyes shot open to watch her light pierce the dark heart of the Sin. Golden light exploded inside it...

And then it was gone.

Asmodeus was no more, and the Sin of Lust was banished to Hell. As her light consumed the last of the Darkness, Alice dropped her hands, extinguishing the golden glow.

Alice had killed the Prince of Hell—the mortal vessel and original form of the fallen archangel—and banished the Sin of Lust to Hell, where it belonged. For, the Sin and Asmodeus were not one and the same. When Asmodeus fell from Grace, he fell by becoming the personification of Lust, allowing the entity of the Sin to fuse into his immortal body. An immortal body that Alice had obliterated.

But Sins were entities, like Virtues, like Darkness, like Spirit. Unkillable, even by a Spirit-wielding witch. And banishment from a Nephilim could not contain the Sin in Hell forever. It would find a way to escape, to seep through the cracks and infect the world, but if it desired a physical body, it could only claim a weak mortal vessel for the rest of eternity. The Sin of Lust would not fight as an immortal fallen angel in the next Apokalypsis War between the Sins and the Virtues three hundred years from now.

A war the immortal Salem Witch would live to fight in.

She had dealt a devastating blow to Hell.

But her Salem War was not yet finished.

She stared at Hathorne, Asmodeus's mortal vessel, a look of disgust disguising her face. Wordlessly, she spun on her heel and marched out of the house, leaving Hathorne where he laid dead in a pile of water from the melted icicle spears.

Although she no longer glowed with earthy green light, Alice's magic was near boundless. The power at her disposal—power from the Creator—was incredible and awe-inspiring, but terrifying at the same time. The havoc she could wreak with this power if she were not careful...

She weaved her way through the town, a silent shadow, moving with deathly silence through the night.

Alice pounded her fist on the wooden door of a large, yet simple wooden home built far from the prying eyes of the town. A house intermittently inhabited by special guests. From inside the home came a deep, male voice, grumbling about people calling on him at this ungodly hour.

The heavy wood door swung open, and a gentleman in his forties appeared in the door frame. He stared at Alice with groggy eyes before it hit him.

Gasping, he dropped his lantern, the glass shattering on impact and sending fire spewing over the wooden doorframe. Alice merely waved her hands, extinguishing the flames without a glance. The gentleman of the house gasped, frantically stumbling backward to flee from Alice. He gripped the door and threw his body weight into it to thrust it close.

Without any change in her expression, Alice merely raised her arm, her palm open and facing the door, then thrust it forward. The gust of wind blowing from her hand was so powerful, it ripped the door off its hinges and slammed into the man, carrying them both down the hall until man and door crashed against the ground.

Striding into the house, Alice flicked her wrist, using her magic to lift the heavy door off the man, but her other hand pointed at him, locking him in place with her magic.

"Hello, Governor," she spoke nonchalantly. "I do believe it is time we have a chat about these witch trials. Do you not agree?"

Governor Sir William Phips stared at Alice in horror.

"Y-you... I-I was t-told you w-were d-dead."

"Yes, well, it did not stick," she said flippantly. "You see, the people were correct, but also wrong. I am not exactly human, but I did not lie either. I am a witch, but I did none of the things I was accused of. You see, Governor, I am the daughter of an angel. You do know what an angel is, do you not?" She raised a single auburn eyebrow.

All he could do was stare at her in disbelief.

"Not that it matters, but I thought it might help you to understand. You see, Governor, I did, in fact, die. But Heaven decided it was not my time yet... or ever," she added in a grumble. "The Creator, Goddess, God, whatever you want to call Him or Her, asked me to return to end these God forsaken trials. So, I did. And now here we are. And do you know why I am here, in your house?"

"N-no," the Governor stammered, trying with all his might to appear unafraid, but his aura stank of terror.

"Because, Governor," Alice practically hissed the title at him, rage flickering in her dark green irises. "You have the power to end these Trials, but you have neglected to save the people you are supposed to protect. So, that leaves us with two options. Or rather, *you* with two options." She raised a single finger. "First option, you continue to ignore the vermin spreading fear throughout the New World, causing mass panic and hysteria and massacring people, and I will burn the entire town to the ground. And then I will do the same to the next town, and the next, and the next."

"Y-you w-would not." He cleared his throat and spoke feebly, "You would not dare."

"Oh, I most certainly would." She grinned manically at him. "And I will raise a new society from the ashes. You have had a taste of what I can do, Governor. That was nothing more than a party trick compared with what I will unleash if you choose this route."

The Governor gulped, his Adam's apple bobbing, but he kept his voice steady. "And what is my other option?"

"I am so glad you asked," Alice mocked. "Your second option is to put an end to these trials. I do not care how you do it, but you will do it and you will ensure this never happens again."

He paled a shade. "And how am I supposed to ensure it never happens again?" he argued.

Alice growled at him, "Like I said, I do not care how you do it, so long as you do accomplish the task. You are a politician. Figure it out." She wagged her finger at him like a naughty puppy. "So... have you made your decision?"

"Option two, please," he squeaked.

"Excellent," Alice said without a smile. "Now, Governor, when you awake in the morning, you will find your wife has been accused of witchcraft. If my warnings have not been enough, perhaps this will spur you to take action."

The Governor balked at her. "What have you done to my wife?"

"Nothing," Alice spoke with deadly calm. "I have not harmed her in any way. But the beasts you have allowed to control this town, nay, this colony, have grown wild and unruly, and your wife will suffer at their hands because of your foolhardiness and indifference." She turned and walked to the door, pausing inside the doorframe to look over her shoulder at the man sprawled on the floor. "Oh, and

Governor, after tonight, you will not see me again, so long as you do as I say. Do not give me a reason to return, do you understand?"

"Yes," the man squeaked.

Satisfied, Alice left the Governor lying on the floor with the door of his house torn off its hinges and thrown aside. He stared after her in shock, and despite her magic no longer holding him in place, he remained rooted in his spot on the floor of his entrance hall.

Pulling on that thread of magic inside her gut, Alice spooked in a flash of green light to the field outside the Putnam estate. Thomas and Ann Senior were inside, along with that heinous daughter of theirs. It would be easy to barricade the doors and ignite a fire.

But Alice was not a murderer. The face of the unknown woman from Corwin's basement flashed through her mind, and nausea twisted her stomach. She never wished to take another life again, even if it was a mercy kill.

Alice would let Amara decide their fates. Who better than Death to dole out their punishments? But that did not mean Alice must suffer their power. If she could not take their wealth or social status, then she would take away the one thing they supposedly feared most—their magic.

And this would not be a simple Binding Spell. No. Alice's powers would remove all traces of magic from the Putnam family lineage. Forever.

In another flash of green, Alice spooked inside, appearing at the base of Putnam's bed. She only needed the patriarch and his wife for what she was about to do. But she wanted them awake and aware. She wanted to see the regret on Putnam's face as he rued the day he crossed her.

Bringing her hands together, Alice clapped her hands slowly, but loudly.

Thomas and Ann shot upright in bed, startled by the sudden noise in the middle of the night.

Ann gasped.

"*You*," Thomas growled.

"Yes, *me*," Alice said with a vindictive smirk. "Did you really think you could kill me and I would not return, Putnam? I am *Nephilim* and the Salem Witch." She spread her arms wide. "Welcome to the Salem War. Turns out, *you* are the villain."

Putnam summoned blue magic to his hand to attack, but with a wave of her hand, Alice killed his magic.

"Do not bother. You are no match for me."

"Wh-what do y-you w-want?" Ann stammered, shaking from fear as she glanced between her husband and Alice.

"What I want?" Alice barked out a humorless laugh. "What I want is my husband alive and next to me. What I want is to resurrect the people you killed in these trials. What I want is to raise my daughter. But I cannot have what I want." Alice cocked her head in a truly demented sight. "But neither can you. Hathorne is dead."

Thomas bristled while Ann paled three shades.

"And these witch hunts are about to come to an end. As is your time among witches."

"You are going to kill us. Eye for an eye."

"No, Putnam," Alice spoke softly, letting her green and gold magic dance around her. "I am not going to kill you. What is the fun of a quick death? No, I can think of much better torture."

"Please, spare us." Ann threw herself out of bed, bowing prostrate to Alice.

Without warning, Alice raised her hands, shooting beams of golden light into Thomas's and Ann's hearts, letting Spirit enact her will.

Gasping, the Putnams' spines arched deeply to the point of painful. Their eyes widened and their mouths hung agape as the magic filled them.

Reaching inside to their souls, Alice found the sliver of light that made witches slightly different from humans, and she pulled, yanking it out of their bodies. Golden light wrapped around their source of magic, and Alice sacrificed it to the Divine in the Heavens above.

"Congratulations, Putnam," Alice sneered. "You finally got your wish. You will no longer be burdened by the weight of witchcraft. No Putnam will possess magic ever again."

"You *witch*!" he screamed, scrambling out of bed to lunge at her.

Wind blew past Alice, tousling her fiery red hair as it slammed against Putnam, forcing him to the floor.

"Let me make this perfectly clear, Putnam. I am graciously allowing you to walk away from this encounter with your life. But I warn you, the next time you attack me, I will ensure your death is a long and torturous one." She leaned over him, her green eyes dark with rage. "I am immortal, thanks to you, so I have plenty of time to draw out your pain. Good luck with your humanity, if you have any."

With a flash of green, Alice spooked from the room to the field outside. Moonlight washed over Alice's body, casting a ghostly pallor over her skin, and she deeply inhaled the crisp September night air. Closing her eyes, her lips twisted into a satisfied smile as she relished the sensation of the night. Slowing, she opened her eyes, and with one last glance at the moon, she disappeared into the dark forest.

Alice's bare feet sank into the mud as she faced east, the orange light of the dawn streaming through the trees as the sun rose above the ocean.

She stood at the northernmost point of Salem, in an abandoned meadow lost to the forest.

Breathing in a slow, steady breath through her nose, Alice summoned the limitless power in her gut. Power that flowed from Heaven above.

This war was not over. It began long before Alice was born, and it would not end in a single night.

Witch hunts, burnings, hangings, and torture of innocent men and women had persisted for too long in the Old World. Even animals were executed for suspicion of being possessed by the Devil as a witch's familiar. It was unfathomably idiotic. The immense popularity of the witch hunts, instigated by Asmodeus, had driven the warped beliefs to drift to the New World. A grave mistake on Asmodeus's behalf. For the New World belonged to her, as all of Earth did, and she would bring an end to his lustful reign of terror.

But tonight was the beginning of the end.

I honor the east's rising sun at dawn,
Breath of the Goddess withdrawn.
By the power of the Salem Witch, hear my prayer,
I call upon the element of air.

The wind blew in a rage, swirling around Alice, whipping her fiery red hair, but otherwise leaving her untouched. She turned to the south.

I honor the south's sacred flame,
Heaven's fire always burning untamed.
By the power of the Salem Witch, grant my desire,
I call upon the element of fire.

Green flames burst to life in a circle around her, the flames stretching out in lines to connect to each other, crisscrossing into a pentacle with Alice at the center.

I honor the west's ancient waters,
Heaven's mother and daughter.
By the power of the Salem Witch, combat the slaughter,
I call upon the element of water.

Storm clouds gathered overhead as rain poured in sheets, but her fire did not extinguish as the elements answered her call.

I honor the North and Mother Earth,
Nature's cycle of death and rebirth.
By the power of the Salem Witch, defend my mirth,

I call upon the element of earth.

The ground rumbled beneath her bare feet, rising into a fearsome earthquake that would surely wake the village. But Alice did not care as she unleashed her beloved element. Rock shifted and animals flocked from the forest to watch her as vines exploded from the ground, growing rapidly from the magic she thrust into the earth.

I honor Heaven above, the Spirit within all,
As above, so below, so the universe, so the soul.
By the power of the Salem Witch, protect my ghost,
I call upon the element of Spirit.

Golden lightning shot from the sky, striking Alice in the chest, coursing down her limbs. Releasing the electrical current from her body, golden lightning crackled across the circle, striking the ground. Alice channeled that raw power to her outstretched palms. The lightning discharged through the clearing, striking a spot in the air. Light exploded from that point, bursting out in a circle.

A portal swirled to life, its colors of green and gold wrapping around each other as though the magic itself were alive.

With golden lightning sparking at her fingertips and an aura of green billowing around her, Alice strode through the portal she created. As she stepped through, her foot touched down on foreign soil, and Alice emerged from the portal into the Old World.

Smiling to herself, Alice snapped her fingers, closing the portal that had transported her across the ocean to Europe.

The time had come to end these witch hunts, and she would start with the demons Asmodeus had summoned from Hell to wreak havoc on Alice's domain. And one by one, they would fall to her magic until not a single demon remained, and then Alice would use the power of Spirit to rid the earth of the soulless humans who propagated the witch hunts that spread to the New World and stole everything from her.

She bowed her head to pray.

Mother Earth, my guardian,
Enlighten the parts of me that dwell in shadow,
Strengthen the parts of me that are weak,
Mend the brokenness I suffer from endless blows,
Grant me a spirit that is strong, not meek,
Renew the peace and love that died within me.

Without looking back, Alice strode into the dark forest.
  This would not take long.

CHAPTER THIRTEEN

WELCOME TO ASYLUM

A caravan pulled by horses, oxen, mules, bulls and heifers, and other farm animals trailed behind Alice as her people huddled inside canvas-covered wagons, sheltered from the fierce winds, their body heat keeping one another warm. A few unfortunate men, and a woman or two, trudged through the snow, guiding the livestock as best they could. Alice's water magic swept the road to pack the late February snow underfoot, keeping the animals and carts getting stuck in the snow as she attempted to warm the air with fire magic.

"Goody," Elizabeth Bradbury shouted as she trudged over the rough terrain, her footing sure as she carried in her arms the bundle of blankets that cocooned Ariel.

Ariel had formed a strong connection with Elizabeth while separated from Alice, and a twinge of jealousy panged Alice's heart, but she knew she had the rest of Ariel's life to make up for it, for Alice would never die.

"People are asking, how far are we? Even with your magic sheltering us, we cannot endure much more of this."

"Trust me," Alice touched a hand to her friend's shoulder. "Trust me to lead our people to a better life. We are almost there. Tell the people it will not be long now."

Elizabeth studied the younger woman, then, with a terse nod, returned to the covered wagons. Alice turned to the path, magic whipping out of her. Fire rushed forth, melting snow into water that was then swept away or absorbed by the earth. Air magic whistled through the air, shifting mounds of snow on the ground while keeping it from piling on the wagons and on the path. Earth magic rushed through the ground beneath their feet, hardening the mud to make the journey easier for the carts and livestock dragging the heavy loads.

Despite her magic, the caravan slowed as they traversed the increasingly difficult terrain of climbing uphill. The hill was slight, but after a long day of hauling cargo, the livestock were tired. Alice continued to cut forward, her magic rushing in all directions to aid the travelers behind her.

As Alice moved forward, the trees of the forest seemed to move out of the way, clearing the way for her as she climbed the hill toward two white oak trees.

Energy slammed into her, and Alice nearly staggered under the force.

Humans. Hundreds—no, thousands—inhabited this land. But she could sense them clearer than she could sense the magic of the witches traveling in her caravan. These humans were strong in Spirit. Their auras were tangible, a pulsing energy hovering around them.

As a deeply tanned, middle-aged Native American man appeared between the two white oak trees, Alice stumbled to a halt, the caravan oblivious to what she sensed and saw.

From behind the man came a middle-aged woman, dressed in the same fur-lined hide clothing that he donned, then a younger woman, not much older than Alice and with hip-length coarse black hair.

With a smile, the young woman beckoned Alice forward. Alice's magic extended toward the woman, searching for her intent, but Alice did not find any maliciousness from the youth, only wariness from the man and woman.

The Chief, Alice realized as she stepped forward. And his wife and daughter. Of course, he was wary of the foreigners intruding on his land. Alice had no idea the tribes extended so far west.

She swallowed the congestion clogging her throat as she climbed toward the three. Alice had communed with the Earth before journeying west. Why would Mother Earth—the very essence of the planet itself—lead her to this place if humans who honored nature lived here? Why not lead her somewhere no one could disturb them?

The young woman smiled warmly at Alice as she closed the distance up the hill, but Alice could only offer an uncertain smile in return.

The Chief spoke something in his native tongue, a language foreign to Alice. As panic rose in her chest, Alice tried to convey that she did not understand. How was she to communicate with them?

The young woman smiled. "Do not worry, Alice, daughter of Uriel. I am Angeni, daughter of the Chief of the Winnebago Tribe and wise woman to the tribe."

Alice stepped back in surprise. "You know who I am?"

"I do. My father says, 'Welcome. We do not wish for war with you and welcome you as guests in our land, but we will not relinquish it.'"

"I do not wish to encroach on your land," Alice said, her heart falling. Where were they supposed to go? All this magic, all this power, enough to kill a Prince of Hell, but she could not lead her people to a new home? "We will move on, but I do not know to where. The Earth led me here, but I do not understand why."

Angeni translated Alice's words to her father, at which he smiled and uncrossed his arms over his chest to offer his left hand to Alice in the traditional witch handshake of respect.

She sighed in relief as she slipped her hand past his to grasp his forearm.

The Chief did not speak, but Angeni said, "The Earth spoke to me and foretold your coming. But what she said, I did not completely understand. The Great Mother has blessed our tribe with the knowledge of Olde Earth Magic, and it has been invaluable. But you are blessed with something more, Daughter of Heaven. You are Nephilim and Salem Witch, a combination never before born. You have the right to call upon your mother at your leisure, but the Earth, She said you must do so when you have found your home. She said it is here, but it is not. I do not know what She means, but perhaps you do."

Alice stared at the young woman. "It is here, but it is not?" Alice repeated the woman's words slowly, then let her eyes drifted beyond the Chief and his family.

When Alice died, hanging from that noose, she had been here... but also... not.

Alice did not want to create a new spiritual plane for her people to live on, although she knew she could, but how could she bear to be separated from earth? But what if...

Reaching for the power swirling in her core, Alice grasped the green and gold light, the power that eternally linked her soul to her mother, and yanked.

Brilliant green light burst to life between Alice and the Chief's family, who stumbled away from the magic, shielding their eyes. The light grew in intensity, but Alice did not look away from the light of Heaven until it faded, revealing a woman with pristine angel wings.

Uriel stood barefoot on the earth, her toes wiggling in the dark soil—the surrounding snow melted from her heavenly presence. Her only garment was a simple, brown leather dress hugging her curvy frame and a leather quiver and bow strapped to her back. Like all angels, she stood a perfect seven-feet tall, and a gene that gave Alice her abnormally tall height of five-foot-eleven.

White apple blossoms wound through her luscious red hair like a veil, falling from the golden wreath of laurel crowning her brow, and she smelled of freshly tilled soil and the sweet scent of wildflowers.

Apple blossoms, Alice realized with a smile. Uriel's symbol represented life continuing after enduring death in the winter of mortal life. And Alice understood. She was truly the daughter of an angel, always destined to be immortal.

"Hello, daughter." Uriel's smile grew as she gazed upon her daughter.

Alice beamed at her mother, her eyes shining with unshed tears. "Mother..." she trailed off, then after clearing her throat, tried again. "Mother... there is someone I want you to meet."

Alice did not look behind her as she waved Elizabeth forward. Elizabeth rushed up the hill, slightly breathless, as she gazed at Uriel. Careful of the bundle in her arms, she bowed to the angel.

"This is my daughter, Ariel," Alice said, taking the bundle containing a sleeping baby girl, about one year of age, with fiery red hair and hunter green eyes.

"Her name is Ariel," Alice whispered. "Ariel Martha."

If possible, Uriel's smile grew wider as she reached down to brush Ariel's forehead. Alice transitioned the baby bundle into Uriel's arms, and Uriel gently rocked the babe, singing a lullaby in a foreign language—Enochian, the language of angels, which Alice understood inherently.

"You know," Uriel said to Alice. "Most angel born mortals and their celestial parents are not as blessed as us. Many of the celestials who sire mortal children are males who mate with human or witch females. While the celestial parent is absent, the mother carries the child to term, then raises the child. But as a female, I carried you to term here on Earth, and as it is my domain, I was permitted to raise you." Looking up, she stared into Alice's eyes as she said, "By the Creator, they were the best three years of my immortal life."

Tears spilled down Alice's cheeks. "I remember," she sobbed. "I do not know how, but somehow, I do. Before I knew I was the Salem Witch, before I knew what it meant to be the daughter of Uriel, all I saw when I closed my eyes at night was you. There were times... I thought I heard voices, but it was you. You were guiding me. You were always with me, watching over me."

Handing Ariel to Alice, Uriel leaned down to touch her forehead to her daughters and whispered, "You should not have had to sacrifice being with your daughter for the first year of her life. You should not have had to sacrifice your mortality. There is so much I wish I could have protected you from, but I could not. Know that I am proud of you, my daughter, as is our Creator. You are loved by Heaven and Earth. Build your asylum, build your home here, and raise your daughter in peace. Use my power and the power of the Salem Witch to charge Angeni's Olde Earth Magic and create the world *you* envision. Spirit will guide you, and it is never wrong. Cherish the years you have with her, and the years you will have with the descendants to come. You may be immortal, but eternity passes in the blink of an eye. I am always with you, Alice. I love you, Daughter of Heaven."

Uriel turned into a ball of brilliant green light that faded as she returned to the heavenly realms.

With a sigh and a sorrowful smile, Alice returned Ariel to Elizabeth's arms, then offered her left hand to Angeni in the traditional witch handshake of respect.

"If you will assist me with your knowledge of Olde Earth Magic, I believe I have a solution for our living arrangements, one that will not impede on your lands. One where we can live together in harmony, as my people will be here, but not physically present, and the land will remain yours."

With a confident smile, Angeni translated Alice's words to her father, who, with a confused expression, said something to Angeni, who merely shrugged.

The Chief sighed with what might have been exasperation, then shook his head. Chuckling lightly, he took his wife by the hand and stepped away from the twin white oak trees, leaving his daughter and Alice alone.

"I am not sure what you are doing exactly, but I trust you, daughter of Uriel, to respect the Earth and Her people."

"I did not become immortal to ruin the lives of others. I became immortal to save them." Alice stepped forward, brushing her waist-length fiery red hair away from her face. She would have to cut it. Alice wore it long, but after death, she was someone new. "Place your hands on my back, please." Angeni did as instructed, her touch feather light.

Placing a hand on each tree trunk, Alice called upon the magic in her blood, her bones, and her flesh, summoning the power of four elements. But the fifth, no, the fifth she called with her soul, and Spirit rushed to answer her. Imagining the world she had experienced in death, Alice allowed her power to fill her.

The Earth rose to meet her, the knowledge of Olde Earth Magic flooding from the Earth through Angeni and into Alice, and Alice understood. She understood how to create the world she sought for her people, a world safe to practice magic, to be the witches they were born to be. A world where they would not fear witchcraft but accept themselves for who they were.

And she let the magic free as she chanted a simple to spell to call her elements.

Air, my breath,
Fire, my heart,
Water, my blood,
Earth, my body,
Spirit, my Eternity.

Green and gold magic burst from Alice's palms. Her magic rushed over the land, spreading in every direction. The white oak trees she touched glowed green and gold with the power of Earth and Spirit. The tops of the oaks stretched toward one another, their branches entwining like fingers of hands until they formed an archway. Alight with earthy magic, the trees grew and grew until they were the size of ancient oaks.

Her hair and eyes turned silver as golden magic burst out of her hand, rushing into the tree arch. The arch absorbed every ounce of magic until the magic erupted. Sparkling green and gold magic flew out of the arch, a wall of green and gold growing in either direction, glittering with the touch of Heavenly Spirit, before it faded. The people in Alice's caravan looked on in shock and wonder, their faces full of awe as they witnessed their leader use her heavenly magic.

The green and gold magic faded, and it was done.

On the outside, nothing appeared different. Alice could see the Chief and his wife, and his people assembled behind him in the village within the woods. But if Alice were to step through the arch... everything would be different.

She had created a different world. A space within a space, protected by wards that were impenetrable except to witches and descendants of the Winnebago tribe.

Alice dropped her hands from the archway as Angeni stepped away. The young wise woman offered Alice a simple nod as she stared at the arch with awe.

"The Great Mother knows the way, and she led you by your faith. May your people be blessed this day, and every day after as long as you honor the Earth."

"I can promise you, as long as I am alive, I will protect this land alongside your people. It shall not perish." Alice turned to the caravan dotting the hill below her. Magically amplifying her voice, she spoke, "My fellow witches, I do not need to tell you what an arduous journey this has been. Had I not told you prior to our departure, yet you followed me, anyway? For many of you, this has been the journey of a lifetime, and for others, you are simply ready to make a new home, find a fresh start far away from the death and destruction suffered in Salem. My friends, I promised you a safe place, a place where we could practice our magic freely, without fear of discovery and persecution. But I promise now, this journey was worth it, for I give you our new home. When you step through this archway, you will find a land untouched, a land hidden from humans except for this tribe, a land where we can be *free*."

Silence permeated the forest. And then... the witches erupted in cheers. Children hopped out of the covered wagons, sprinting for the archway. Men and women burst into tears, their relief too much to contain. The caravan moved forward with renewed strength, knowing their final destination was within reach.

Elizabeth offered Ariel to Alice, and for the first time since Alice lost her husband, she smiled with unconcealed happiness as she rocked her daughter in her arms and passed through the arch into Asylum. Green and gold magic swirled around the mother and daughter, but Alice did not notice. She was so lost in her daughter's hunter green eyes.

And then she felt it. The feeling of his soul returning to this world.

"John," she breathed his name. Her soulmate had been reborn. "I will find you. In this lifetime and the next, and every time after that until we are immortal together." She gazed at the daughter born to both of them.

"Welcome to Asylum."

ALICE PARKER'S FAMILY NEVER FILED A PETITION FOR RESTITUTION AND FOR HER NAME TO BE CLEARED.

ALICE PARKER'S CONVICTION WAS OVERTURNED ON OCTOBER 31ST, 2001, ALONG WITH BRIDGET BISHOP, SUSANNA MARTIN, WILMOT REDD, AND MARGARET SCOTT. ANN PUDEATOR WAS CLEARED IN 1957. ALL OTHER WITCHES WERE CLEARED ON OCTOBER 17TH, 1711 BY THE STATE OF MASSACHUSETTS.

ALICE PARKER IS REMEMBERED IN THE SALEM WITCH TRIALS MEMORIAL, 1992, AND PROCTOR'S LEDGE MEMORIAL, 2017.

BOOK ONE: THE LOST WITCH

Five deadly Trials. An ancient, sinister evil.

**One lost witch
with the power to save the world.**

Welcome to Asylum.

Twelve-year-old Hayden Black has never been normal, that much she knew, but when her father is abducted by demons, she learns just how remarkable she truly is. Not only is she a witch, but Heaven's angels have chosen her as the next Salem Witch, destined to protect the world from evil... if she can survive the deadly Salem Witch Trials first.

Now Hayden must traverse the magical world of Asylum and learn to use her powers. If she does not master all five elements — air, fire, water, earth, and Spirit — before her seventeenth birthday, she forfeits her life.

Hayden might have started her journey orphaned and alone, but it does not take her long to forge new friendships and attract new enemies. Hayden thought her only nemesis was the residential bully, but her greatest enemy, a terrible evil lurking in the shadows, has yet to reveal itself.

Will Hayden master her air magic in time to save her friends and find her father? Or will she perish alongside them?

The Lost Witch is the first book in an urban fantasy series intended for readers ages ten and above who love Percy Jackson and Avatar: The Last Airbender.

Help Me Out

Thank you for reading Hayden Black and the Salem Witch Trials: Prequel Novella! Before you begin Hayden's adventure the world of Asylum in Book One: The Lost Witch, please leave a review for The Salem Witch.

Scan this QR code to leave a review:

Sign Up For My Author Newsletter

Subscribe to my newsletter to receive book updates and exclusive bonus content, including a free short story from Jamie's perspective of Hayden's disastrous arrival.

Jamie Bishop is bored. Bored with school. Bored with training. Bored with Asylum.

But adventure is coming...

Or scan the QR code to read on Amazon today!

ABOUT THE AUTHOR
B. C. TAYLOR

Click here to view a full list of B. C. Taylor's published and upcoming novels.

Visit her on the web at:

Website: https://www.brooklynctaylor.com
Instagram: https://www.instagram.com/brooklyn_tay
Goodreads:
https://www.goodreads.com/user/show/155122248-brooklyn-taylor
Pinterest: https://www.pinterest.com/brooklyn_tay7/
Facebook Page:
https://www.facebook.com/profile.php?id=100084524515084

B. C. Taylor grew up in small town Salem, Wisconsin, alongside her loyal yellow Labrador, Salem. Her passion for witches and magic sparked at a young age, as did her love for reading and world mythology. Since the fifth grade, B. C. Taylor wanted to be a writer, but being a total nerd, her equal passions for science and math drove her to study engineering at the University of Wisconsin — Madison. Soon after graduating, she began writing stories again, and Hayden Black consumed every spare moment of her time. When she's not writing or designing cars at her day job, B. C. Taylor can be found swimming, paddle boarding, or keeping her boxing skills sharp.

She invites readers to get first looks, exclusive content, and more by subscribing to her newsletter:

Acknowledgements

Since The Salem Witch is a fantasy novella based on historical events, it is only appropriate that I acknowledge the men and women who lost their lives to the 1692 Salem Witch Trials and in the witch hunts rampant across Europe for centuries before. Those who forget history are doomed to repeat it—may we never relive the events of this dark time in human history.

Second, I want to acknowledge all the wonderful friends and family who have supported me in writing Hayden's story so that I could write Kova's backstory. I am so thankful for each of you supporting this part of my life because it truly brings me so much happiness.

To all the fans who asked for Kova's story, this one is for you! While I had to condense the Trials into a single book, I hope her adventure did not disappoint. Thank you for being such super fans. I cannot express enough how much I love hearing from my fans! And stay tuned... this isn't the last you'll read from the World of Asylum. As a fully realized Salem Witch, it's Hayden's turn to mentor other witches in the sequel Dani Sanchez and the Seven Deadly Sins.

Lastly, I want to give thanks to God, for granting me so many opportunities in life to pursue what I love and for the adventure of travel, during which I finished writing this novella. My life isn't perfect, but I wouldn't give up my experiences for anything. I look forward to where in the world you are leading me next.